C000199911

Strokes of Genius

Vol. 1

Kitty von Klass

Published in 2011 by Damn Dirty Fiction

First Edition

To my lovely parents for having me.
To my wonderful family for putting up with me.
And to all the dirty, filthy guys that inspire me.

Table of Contents

1. Red Mac   Page 9

2. Watching you   Page 17

3. My first Spit Roast   Page 23

4. The flicks   Page 33

5. Make me beg   Page 39

6. The velvet room   Page 47

7. Back to mine   Page 55

8. Sweet ass Candy   Page 65

Red Mac

I sigh looking out the open window. The rain pelts down outside and shows no sign of stopping. Good. I love the rain. It makes me horny. I inhale deeply, the scent of salt and grass mingling with my sex as I bring my wet fingers to my mouth and suck off my pussy juice.

My cunt throbs and feels empty. I stare at my dildo but it's just not enough, what I need right now is some cock. The rain drives me crazy. Whenever it rains I just need a big hard shaft in me. Nothing else will do.

I glance out the window, and that's when I see you. I love to pleasure myself in full view of the street, and every now and again someone like you gets a lucky break, a full on gymnastic performance, but not today, today I need something more than just the thought of our tongues dancing together furiously, imagining it's your hands running the length of my body, touching my breasts and tweaking my nipples until they're rock hard, begging to be sucked into a hot warm mouth and licked and flicked and bitten.

You're still staring when I return my gaze out the window, a bemused but desperate look on your face. I notice that your arms are not in the sleeves of your rain coat, they're buried deep inside it. Are you stroking your cock while you're looking at me? Were you close to cumming and I spoilt it for you?

I lean up on my elbows so you can see my huge full breasts, and you smile. Your cheeks flush as you realise you've been seen, but mine don't. I like to be watched, but I also like to fuck. Your coat swings open. I see your erect cock, and it's beautiful.

I lick my lips, an unconscious reaction, and I blush when I realise. You smile wide as you push your cock back in your boxers and do up your fly, beckoning me. Do you want me to come out there? I mouth at you, gesturing with my hands, and you nod, a wry smile on your face.

I sit up further so you can see the curve of my waist and arse, and you rub your cock through your trousers. Is it aching? Does it want to fuck me? I think it does.

I lean forward and peer out the window, the street is practically empty and the park across the road from me, even more so. We'll have plenty of uninterrupted time, and God, my pussy is aching.

I nod and pull back from the window as I shut it. I wonder about dressing, but it's pissing down and everything will be off again pretty quickly because I'm so damn horny, so I just grab my long red rain mac, and some red heels, and I'm out the door before I have the chance to change my mind.

You're waiting right at the entrance to the apartment building, soaked to the skin, and sexy as hell. Your eyes tell me you're just as horny as I am, they're filled with the kind of hunger you can never hope to satiate. There's a flash of recognition between us before I pull you into the hallway, just out of sight of the street, parting my mac so you can see I'm naked underneath.

Your eyes grow huge and you snarl as you tip your head down and suck my breast into your mouth. This is fucking crazy, but at this precise moment I don't even care. Your tongue flicks hard against my nipple and your teeth join it gently, teasingly. I think I might cum just from that, but I clench my pussy to stop it. You must feel me tense because you smile.

"You like that?" you whisper, and I nod, a low moan emitting from my mouth when I part my lips to speak. I don't have time to answer because I feel your hands creep over my stomach and down to that aching spot between my legs, that trembling hole that needs to be filled so desperately with whatever you want to put in it.

There's a tentative finger against my clit, my legs tremble and I have trouble staying standing as you begin to rub it, gently at first in long slow strokes, dipping just inside my pussy as you rock it back and forth in a consistent rhythm.
God that's so good.

Then I feel your fingers inside me, hooking forwards at the entrance to find my g-spot, and they're just the right length, like they were made to fuck me like this, and as your palm finds its way onto my clit I can't control my legs and have to grab hold of your hair and shoulder to keep standing as I arch into your hand, and you fuck me with it deep and hard.

"That... is so fine," I mumble into your ear as I lean forward, trying to keep my balance, and I try to hold back but I'm just too horny right now. I arch against the wall and groan long and hard as my pussy clenches around your fingers before I cum. My orgasm so hard and powerful, my legs give way and you have to grab me around the arse to stop me from falling.

Pushing me back against the wall, you get on your knees and lap at my pussy. It's way too intense. I try to push you back but you don't stop, burying your face in-between my thighs and lapping every bit of juice like you're trying to eat me.

My fingers are rough in your hair, and I tug you relentlessly as I try to writhe away. You don't budge and if I thought your fingers were good, they had nothing on your tongue, that long insistent stroke that you use, forcing me to buck against your face. You really are very good at this, but I want to pleasure you now, it seems only fair.

I pull your head back forcefully, stroking your cheek after, as way of apology. You look disappointed until I pull you up to my mouth and kiss you hard, all the while unzipping your fly and prying your cock out of your boxers. The taste of me is ripe on your lips, and I bite them gently as I kiss you.

Your cock falls free, rock hard and rubbing against my thighs. Are you covering yourself in the juice dripping from between my legs? You nudge against my clit and let out a sigh as you kiss me. I bet you want to be in that dripping wet cunt? I bet you want to feel how tight and hot it is as you slip your cock in there?

All in good time.

I pull you towards me and then push you against the wall before you have time to protest, unbuttoning your shirt slowly. You groan as you lean your head back. I'm torturing you right now and I know it, but it will be worth it.

I kiss you hard on the mouth before pulling away and running my tongue across your chest. I circle your nipple and watch your hands tense into fists against the wall. Pulling it hard in my mouth, I bite it gently. The sound you make gets me so wet I do it again and again. Licking and teasing and then biting, this time with more force.

Your knuckles are white as your whole body tenses. Enough teasing I think. I work my way down across your abs, sweeping my tongue back and forwards until I reach your cock, jutting hard from your body.

I take the tip into my mouth, running my tongue across the top and gently nudging your foreskin down so I don't hurt you. Once your proud head is fully exposed I tease you gently, licking in long strokes over the top and then down the shaft, over the top and then down the shaft. Your groans get louder.

I warn you with my eyes glancing to the entrance way to number 1. You're fazed for a moment until you work it out and clamp your lips shut. Still working the tip I feel your hand on the back of my head. You want me to suck it deep now I'm guessing? Your hands grip

11

my hair and gently push my mouth further down your shaft. I don't fight you, I want to suck you deep, feel the whole of your huge cock in my throat. You're probably big enough to make me gag completely but I try to relax as best I can as I take you all in and then suck with everything I have in me.

I move back and forth, slowly at first, long deep sucks, wet lips and tongue teasing the head as I pull you out completely before swallowing you again. My pussy is dripping thinking of this huge beast inside me. You grip my hair as you watch me sucking your cock, your hips arching off the wall to meet me at each stroke.

I reach up my hand and cup your balls, raking my fingernails over and massaging them, and I think you're going to cum right then but you hold my head still for a moment to regain composure. I'm guessing you liked that a lot?

I move my hand to your shaft and work it while I suck and lick the head.

"That is so fucking hot," you blurt out.

I hear the internal lock to number one click and I freeze. The door handle turns and I stand abruptly, pushing your cock back into your coat and closing mine in one swift movement.

"Morning Mrs. James," I smile sweetly.

She shuffles into the hallway. Fuck, she's getting her post. I don't have time for this shit.

I grab your hand and pull you towards the exit, slamming the door behind us. We're both giggling as we run across the street, you trying to hold up your trousers and keep your cock contained beneath your mac, and me trying to balance in these stupid heels, with legs that you've turned to jelly with your skilful tongue and hands.

The park's empty, aside from an old gent walking his dog. He doesn't look like he'd mind a show but I don't fancy getting arrested today so I push you backwards towards the trees and we duck inside. You try to stop me, but I don't let you, tugging you harder and deeper into the thicket.

You stop.

"Not here." I shake my head.

I reach the spot I was heading for, an opening in the centre, the rain is still pounding. You hesitate in the treeline.

"I want you to fuck me in the rain," I demand, and your smile is wicked. You look pretty game for anything right now.

12

Glancing about, I'm nervous as I remove my mac standing in front of you completely naked, but no other idiots are going to be out here in this weather, I don't think we need to worry about it, and you seem to come to the same conclusion because you're out of your coat and shirt, and yanking down your trousers, quicker than I could have done it. I thought I was horny, but I guess I left you a bit blue-balled, and as you take off your boxers my suspicions are confirmed.

You look unsure of what to do with your shoes as you look at them and then at me. I shrug, I kept mine on. You laugh. I think you decided to keep yours on too. I'm pleased, they'll probably give you a better grip for that ripe fucking you're going to give me.

I go to kneel in front of you but you shake your head. I'm confused, don't you want me to suck you some more? You pull me to you and kiss me hard. I feel your cock against my stomach and push into it, twisting to give you some sensation, and you yell harder than you did inside, it's animalistic and it makes me drip. Your hands are in my hair as you kiss me, and then they snake down my back, smacking my arse hard, before you grab it with both hands and ease me off the floor.

I cling around your neck and use my thighs to grip around your waist. You're really strong. I can feel the tight muscles of your arms against my waist. I admire your confidence. I think we're going to have to lean against something eventually, but that doesn't stop you. You nudge against my clit with your hard cock and I feel ripples tingling from my pussy right up to my head.

Your eyes question mine. Are you wondering if I'm still okay with this, or are you just savouring the moment?

I arch up and slide myself onto your cock. It's so big it actually hurts at first but you're gentle taking it slowly until I stretch to accommodate you.

I grip hard with my thighs, my arms tight around your back as you fill me, but it's slow and steady and the rhythm feels so good. We're both soaking wet, our kisses deep and hard, tasting the salt of each other's tongues mixed with the heady rain. Our bodies slip and slide but it only makes it more fun.

"mmmmm," I moan right in your ear.

You close your eyes and work against me still slow and steady, holding me tight around the arse, but I feel your need to work me harder, each thrust more urgent than the last and your face tight with tension.

13

You stumble with me still clamped around your waist and your cock still buried deep inside my hot, dripping pussy. The angle of your movement brushing your pelvis against my clit is driving me nuts, but it's too hard for us to move like this and reluctantly you signal for me to release your waist, which I do, and you let me down.

I glance about. A fallen tree looks the perfect height. I move towards it and bend over, spreading my legs wide to offer you my pussy to do with as you will. You tease me with the head of your cock, rubbing it against my arse and then in sweeping movements to my clit and back again before you take me by surprise and ram it into me all the way to the hilt.

I gasp as you pull back on my hips so you can drive yourself into me as deep as you can get and there's nothing slow and steady about this now. This is a seriously hard and deep fucking. The bark of the tree scratches my skin and causes pain, but I like it combined with the ramming of your cock against me and your hands tight on my hips, pulling me back with each desperate thrust, faster and harder.

Still you seem to need to be deeper as you reach forwards and grab my shoulders, pulling me back into you, and I clamp my throbbing pussy around your cock to increase our pleasure.

I feel you're close and so am I, reaching down I stroke my clit in long steady strokes, just how I like it. I can barely keep my hands in place, as you're banging me so hard I think you might break me, but it feels amazing to have you buried deep into my dripping, hot pussy.

The feel of the rain on my skin and in my mouth, the bark of the tree scratching against the front of my hips, my hand on my clit working feverishly now as I'm close, and I can tell by your moans that you are too. Our sounds are guttural, unconscious, and I let out a cry as I cum hard on your cock, my whole body exploding with sensation, pulses gliding from my core to my toes, and my limbs shaking.

"Fuck," you moan as you pull back hard, stop, and then pull back on me again, and I feel your cock tighten before you shoot your hot spunk into me, your nails digging into my arse cheeks. I look back to watch your face. It's so hot to see how I've made you feel as you cum inside me, your body still shuddering with release as you pull back and wipe the rain from your face.

I'm barely able to stand from the force of the fucking, but I manage to stumble to my coat and put it on as you get dressed. I feel the hot slick of your spunk running down my thighs as we push back

14

through the thicket and out towards the road. It makes me giggle, and I lick my lips like a cat that's had all the cream it can handle.

We reach my door and you smile before walking away.

Turning back you say, "You know we're going to get caught doing that one of these rainy days."

"Yeah but it will be worth it." I reply.

Watching you

Your lips move down her neck and she shudders against you, her arms stretched above her head like a cat, her body twisting and contorting as you work your way further down until you reach her bra, taking a nipple in-between your teeth and biting it to a peak. Her moans echo in the cavernous space but she doesn't try to mask them, she thinks you're alone in here.

She sits up and you lean over her shoulder dotting kisses along the line of her bra strap before unhooking it. She holds it to her for a second, a coy look on her face as she lets one strap fall and then the other, gracefully releasing her breasts, and tossing her bra to the side.

My breath quickens as I look at her dark glossy skin picked out from the light of the window, every curve amplified, hungrily feasted on by your eyes, but also by mine. Her breasts are so very different to my own, small, perky, neat. I bet they feel light like feathers when you cup them in your hands.

Her nipples are small but the colour of cherries. I lick my lips, wondering what it would be like to run my tongue over her, suck her into my hot wet mouth, trace lazy trails across her skin, tasting the sweet, salty delight that hides in her dark places, just like you are now. I expect she's so very soft when you touch her.

I try to imagine what it feels like for you as you glide your hand down her stomach and over her hips. Her legs are long and lean, with the faintest traces of blonde hair on her tanned thighs, and her feet arch as you kiss down to one of them, and then suck a toe into your mouth. She bites the back of her hand to stifle a moan, but it's still audible and unmistakable in its pleasure. I feel my pussy engorge with juice, my nipples taught and tingling, my body longing for your touch, her touch, any touch. My eyes want to look away but I'm unable to.

This is what I came for.

She giggles as you lick the base of her foot, your tongue slicing up her leg, past her knee, over the tight skin of her inner thigh, pushing her skirt up until her white lace knickers are revealed, straining to contain her sex. I sniff the air, wishing I could inhale her like you are right now, wishing it was my head between her thighs licking over her knickers. I stand on tiptoes so I can see you both better, the outline of her pussy lips clearly visible as you nudge her with your nose and tongue, a wet patch growing around your face.

I bet she smells so sweet.

I slide my hand in my shirt, rub my nipple through my bra until it's hard and hurting, the lace causing friction and allowing me to imagine it's you that's touching me. I almost gasp when you push her underwear to one side revealing her glorious pussy, so very wet, red and inviting. Good enough to eat and so very fuckable. I bet you're trembling with excitement gazing at her pussy, how much do you want to fuck her right now? As much as I want to watch you do it?

Your tongue's tentative, flicking her clit with what looks like lightest pressure until she arches her back off the table, her knuckles white as she grips the edge, her breath fragmented, hard and fast. Your tongue moves faster now, back to front and then side to side and her moans increase in intensity, her back arched so much she must be in pain, but her face shows only pleasure.

My cunt throbs with neglect, my breath almost as fast as hers as I reach inside my bra and pinch my nipple hard, stifling my moan by biting down on my free hand, feeling wet trickling from me, soaking my knickers, my legs starting to tremble.

One of her hands is hard in your hair as she pulls you against her pussy, grinding into your face, her feet pushing against the table to drive you further into her wetness. With your whole head buried between her thighs, her moans of pleasure are my only indication that she's close. Is she clamping around your hand, gripping you tightly with her cunt, her body shaking against you? I wonder how much you want to fuck her right now, I expect with everything in you, but I also know you'll want to make her cum on your face. You're relentless in your need to deliver pleasure and there's no way you'll stop now, she's so close. I recognise the pleasure in her sighs, and I smile as I watch her face, a look of intense pain and concentration plain, even though her eyes are closed, but her lips in a half smile, her tongue darting out across them as she struggles to breathe.

I slide my hand inside the waistband of my skirt, rubbing against the soaking spot in my knickers, the lace scraping against my clit, tingling, tantalising, tempting. So close yet so far removed. I watch with a sigh as you tease the entrance of her pussy with your fingers, pushing inside a fraction and then pulling out. Your face is relaxed as you probe her, you know exactly what you're doing, each time sinking your fingers a little bit further, and taking her a little bit closer to the edge.

I slide my hand inside my knickers and feel the hot wet entrance to my hole. It quivers as I run my fingers around the edge, mirroring your movements on her, sinking them in just a little and pulling out, pushing in further, rubbing my thumb over my clit, as I watch your tongue flicking hers with jealousy. I lean over the shelf to keep my balance as my fingers push in further and further until I'm clamped down on my hand.

Her moans are fast and sharp, and you fuck her hard with three fingers, lapping at her juice which is covering your face and chin. I know how exciting it must be to have her at your mercy, writhing around on the desk, ready to explode in your face any… second… now.

I watch her stomach contract and she throws her head back, a strange gargle emitting from her throat followed by "Fuck, Fuck, Fuck…" Her legs grip around your back and you stop moving for a moment as she cums, pulling on your hair like she wants to yank it out. My eyes dart between you both, the pleasure easy to spot on you equally. Pulling away, you wipe your chin before turning in my direction with a smile and a wink.

Fuck! You know I'm here. You know and you carried on regardless. The thought of it makes me so horny I have to sit on the edge of the desk to keep from toppling over.

She licks her juice from your face as she sits up to kiss you, her hand tugging your shirt frantically out of your trousers and unbuttoning it at the same time, pushing it off your shoulders and sending it to the floor. She smiles up at you as she bites your nipple into her mouth and tugs on it, her hands undoing your belt, your fly, and sliding inside your boxers.

You grunt as she rubs over the end of your cock. I know you must be about ready to explode right now after licking her cunt, but I hope you don't just fuck her, I want to watch her suck you. You kiss her shoulder to hide the fact you're looking at me as she releases you, taking your rock hard cock in her hand and wanking you slowly. You grip the table, no doubt to keep your balance. Your cock's huge, your balls swollen with spunk. I can't wait to watch you unload that all over her.

I stroke my clit with more force as I watch her push you back from the table, sliding off onto her knees in front of you. I can see how fast your breath is coming, how tense your back and legs look as she hesitates with your cock against her mouth, reaching up and cupping your balls, sticking out her tongue…

19

My pussy contracts around my fingers as she licks your head, lapping you with speed, slobbering on your cock as she gobbles it into her mouth, pulling away and licking the shaft and occasionally your balls. You hold her hair back so we can both watch her work. I fuck my fingers frantically, wishing it was me sucking you right now, ready to feel your spunk in my mouth or over my face.

Your body's rigid, your hand tight in her hair, but I know you won't cum yet, that pussy is far too beautiful not to be fucked. You hold her head still pulling your cock out of her mouth. She stands, undoing her skirt and pushing it down with her knickers, stepping out of them both. You pause for a second, are you working out which position to fuck her in? Which position will give me the best view?

She grins, turning away from you and leaning her elbows onto on the desk, her pussy just visible between her thighs as she shakes her ass.

I smile as wide as you do.

My pussy contracts around my fingers again, desperate for release, but I pause for a moment to calm down, I don't want to cum just yet.

You lick down her back, spreading her arse cheeks wide before you stick out your tongue and rim her. She looks concerned. Perhaps she's never been rimmed before?

You don't stop, lapping and dipping your tongue into her arse. I sigh with need, the throbbing between my legs starting to hurt. After a moment her face mellows and she leans her head against the table, her body visibly relaxing. I think she's decided she likes that.

You suck on your finger and tease her with it, probing her arse with your tongue as your fingers slide into her pussy. She lets out a low groan as she bangs the table with her palms. She looks about ready to explode again right now.

I try to control my breath as you square up to her pussy, teasing her with your cock. Her eyes are closed so she doesn't see you turn to me and smile as you inch into her, taking your time, pushing in so I can watch every second as if in slow motion, watch your cock disappear inside her as you drive all the way in and then close your eyes.

I wonder how wet her pussy is, and if she's tight?

It's so horny I want to cum right that second.

I slide my fingers into my pussy, rubbing my clit with my thumb and occasionally pinching a nipple with my free hand.

You grip the edge of the desk as you fuck her, and despite her begging you to go faster and harder you fuck her slowly, allowing me full view of your shaft as it glides in and out teasing her to distraction, teasing me even more. My body starts to shudder as I fuck my hand, wishing more than anything that it was your cock, wanting to feel your length deep inside me, filling me up, fucking me until I beg you as much as she is right now.

"Fuck me harder," she shouts at you and you laugh, yanking her hips back towards you and giving her what she wants. The table lunges forwards as you pound into her, her moans turning to loud pants, her head banging on the table with the force of you ramming into her. You yank on her hair and she smiles as you do. I like that too. I can hear your balls slapping against her thighs, the table scraping against the floor as you fuck her harder and faster, your face tight with tension.

You look close, are you close now?

I rub my clit frantically, my fingers working hard, my hand starting to ache and cramp with the force that I'm using, trying to match the thrusts of your cock in her. Imagining it's me on that table, gripping the edges tight as you bang into me, your hand yanking my hair, the table scraping against my thighs, my pussy clamping around you, ready to explode.

She almost howls her approval as she cums, banging her hand on the table and screaming, and you growl as you drive up into her harder than looks possible. My legs are tense and hurting as I grind on my hand desperate for my own release, my eyes wanting to absorb every second wanting it to be over, but also to last forever.

You slap her as you withdraw, growling as you shoot your spunk over her arse and back. I lick my lips wishing you were covering my face with that glorious cream, and the thought of it is enough to send me over the edge, my orgasm gripping me with force as I watch your spunk splash up her back.

Pulses glide through my rigid body, my legs weak and my arms trembling with the force. I lie back on the desk and close my eyes, struggling to control my breath as remove my hand from my pussy, the last ripples still gripping my insides, and lick my fingers.

"Same time again next week?" I hear you ask her.

"For sure," we both answer in unison.

My first spit roast

You're both already at the bar when I arrive. It's hot today and I'm sweating a little. It trickles between my breasts and runs down my stomach. You smile at me waving your hand, and I motion that I've seen you and head your way.

My emerald wrap dress clings to my curves and I feel it brushing against my suspender belt as I move. I'm nervous as hell as I feel both of you watching my every move, but it eases as I cross the room.

I've never really thought about how good looking your friend Rich is, but now I'm seeing him with different eyes I have to admit he's really something. I catch myself licking my lips as I run my gaze down his shirt to his jeans, excited about what might be lingering beneath his clothes.

You've picked a booth for us to sit in, it's secluded but still visible from the rest of the bar if anyone choses to look in our direction. My breath comes quickly as I reach the table. You lean in and kiss me, and you must realise how nervous I am because you whisper, "Just relax and enjoy this," before you kiss me again.

My lips linger on yours, and I tense a little as I feel Rich's hand on my waist, leaning in and kissing me on the neck. The thrill of two pairs of lips on me makes me wet in an instant. I turn and stare at Rich, his blue eyes drowning me, his hand wandering down my chest and over my nipple, straining at the lace of my bra, and so aroused it hurts. I can feel both your rock hard cocks as I stand sandwiched in-between you, and I struggle to breathe.

Is it really, really hot in here or is it me?

You step back and slide into the booth, and I sit next to you. The cool leather feels nice against the tops of my thighs and arse. Rich pours us champagne before sitting next to me, the pair of you practically crushing me between you. I swallow hard before grabbing a glass of champagne and downing it in one.

Your hand catches mine on the way to put down my glass. Bringing it to your mouth you kiss the inside of my wrist. "Relax, I'm totally fine with this and so is Rich, just enjoy it, tonight is all about you."

I take a few deep breaths and try to relax. I don't want my nerves to spoil it for everyone. We've been talking about this for months, but I still don't understand why you would want to do this. It makes no sense to me, and I can't comprehend how you won't be jealous, but when I reach under the table, stroke your cock through your jeans and feel how hard you are, I know you must really want this because you're like rock.

Rich pours me another glass of champagne and I sip it slowly this time, running my tongue across the rim imagining what's going to happen when you both get me upstairs. How it's going to feel to have two pairs of lips, four hands and two cocks to pleasure me all night. I shiver as I feel your hand on my thigh, toying with the top of my stockings and brushing the bare skin above, and I positively shake when Rich does the same, teasing in circles, working his way further up my thigh, brushing against my sopping wet knickers.

You pull up my dress so I'm exposed and I watch your face as Rich's hand moves inside my underwear, his fingers brushing over my bush before reaching my clit and stroking it gently. You grin, but your eyes look hungry to see more and you peel my knickers down to expose me fully.

I sip my drink, trying to relax my face. No-one's really looking in our direction but if they did right now it would be difficult for them to miss my flushed red cheeks and chest, and the slight waver on my lips as Rich delivers my clit exquisite pleasure. When I feel your fingers join his, searching out my tight wet hole, I let out a groan that sounds deafening, and you must think the same thing because you clamp your lips against mine and deliver a deep kiss as you push your finger inside.

Pulling away from me you lean into Rich as if you're discussing something between you, and I feel you both reach inside my dress, slipping in my bra and teasing it down over my nipples to reveal them. I jump a little as you pinch one between your fingers pushing deeper inside my dripping cunt. I let out another groan and am vaguely aware that you're talking to Rich, but my heart hammering in my ears is too loud for me to make out what you're saying.

It's Rich's lips on mine now, his tongue tastes salty and his kiss is insistent and aggressive as his finger works my clit faster. He pulls back from me quickly and knocks the glass of champagne in my hand, spilling it down my breasts and dress. I'm shocked when I feel your tongue licking it off me. We're right in the middle of the bar someone is going to notice you licking my tits.

24

I glance about nervously but no-one's looking at all. I feel myself relax again and let out a whimper as your mouth meets my nipple and sucks it long and hard before you pull away and turn to Rich.

"She's really dripping now I think we need to get her back to the room before she cums right here at the table, because she'll scream the house down."

"So she's a screamer then?" Rich asks, turning to you with a smile, and you grin.

I don't know how I stand let along make it through the lobby, my legs are like jelly and my pussy's so wet I can feel it trickling down my thighs, even with my knickers still on. You don't let me adjust my bra so my nipples, still rock hard, are now jutting through my dress. I feel ashamed as we walk through the lobby and all the men stare at me, but you seem to really enjoy it, a broad smile on your face and a spring in your step.

What must they think of me? It's obvious I'm going up to a room with two guys, my dress soaked with champagne, my nipples rock hard and my face flushed red. I bet they all think I'm some kind of slut, off to get a good hard fucking. I can't pretend it doesn't turn me on because it does.

Both of your lips are against my body as soon as the lift door shuts, Rich sucking and pinching my tits and you finger fucking me. It feel so good that even when I hear the faint sounds of the camera as the cctv operator no doubt zooms in for some close up, I don't even care.

Rich puts the key in the lock and opens the door. My head's spinning a little from the champagne, and I'm wobbly as I make it to the bed and sit on the edge. Rich crosses the room to the window and closes the curtains, putting on the bedside lamp so the room is bathed in just the right amount of light to see.

You don't waste your time, pulling me up from the bed and untying my dress then spinning me around to face Rich who slips it off my shoulders, pushing it down my arms and leaning in to kiss my neck as he does so. His mouth's red hot against my skin, perhaps because I feel so dirty when he kisses me, like your little slut being pimped out to your friends. He moves up and kisses my lips and I hold around his neck and let my tongue wander in his mouth as you kiss and lick down my spine.

25

I can tell you've removed your t-shirt when you pull away and then brush up against my back, undoing my bra and letting it fall to the floor. Rich starts to unbutton his shirt but I stop him. I think you'd like it more if I undress him? I turn to you with a questioning face, and you nod and smile at me.

I undo his shirt slowly, teasing my fingers just inside and brushing his smooth chest. He grins as I catch his nipple with a nail accidently-on-purpose. Undoing his cuffs, I tug the shirt from him and throw it to the corner of the room. I slide off his belt, making sure I graze his cock often with my wrists and hands as I do, and he squirms a little, brushing his fingers through my hair. I don't turn, but I can hear you undoing your fly and taking your jeans off. I know your boxers have joined them when I feel your cock against my buttocks as you reach your hands around and grab my tits, pulling on the nipples.

I slide off Rich's jeans and his cock is huge, I gasp at the sight of it muttering, "Fuck that's a monster," and crouch down to get a better look.

You bend down and whisper in my ear, "and that's going to be fucking you soon."

I feel my insides turn to jelly and without thinking I take Rich's cock in my hands and start teasing the head with my tongue, wanking it slowly into my lips. He groans as he holds onto my shoulder.

"Fuck, she sucks cock really well."

"I know," you answer and I can tell you're grinning from the pitch of your voice.

I feel you behind me, "That's it baby, suck his cock. Make it really hard baby, suck it good so he can fuck you with it."

I suck Rich's cock as hard as I can and he moans with each thrust into my mouth. You stand patiently for a second but I glance at you and notice you're leaking pre-cum everywhere, you must be crazy horny.

You pull my head back off of Rich's cock and position me on the bed so I'm lying face upwards with my hips on the edge and my feet on the floor. Rich positions himself in-between my thighs and I feel his stubble scratching the tops of my stockings as he uses his teeth to pull off my knickers.

You straddle my chest facing away from me so I can't see what's going on, but I can reach your beautiful arse, and I arch up and bite it gently. You turn and smile at me as I start to rim you, my tongue probing and licking your hole with fervour.

I can feel fingers against my clit but I have no idea if it's you or Rich, until they move with the long strokes I love, and then I know it's you, because only you can pleasure me like that. I shudder when I feel a wet tongue up my thigh and then pushing inside my pussy. Rich's tongue is so long, it feels like a dirty wet cock fucking me right now as you tease and pinch my clit.

I feel like such a slut with you both working on me, but it feels so good. You scoot back up my body and your balls knock against my chin as you place them over my mouth. I suck them in, slurping your balls as Rich starts licking my clit and pushes his fingers into my tight pussy. I moan against your ball sack. Rich is really good at this, in fact he's amazing. He flicks his tongue and fucks me with his fingers and I groan again and again.

You climb off me, I'm disappointed as I wanted to rim your arse some more, but you lie down next to me and tweak my nipples as Rich continues to work on my clit and pussy.

"You're such a slut," you say to me, and I nod because right now I am. "Tell me what a slut you are?" you demand, an aggressive tone in your voice.

"I'm such a slut, such a dirty little slut. I'm loving having your mate lick and finger fuck me right now and I want his cock as well, I want him to fuck me with that huge cock of his, pound my pussy with his big hard cock."

"Fuck babe, that's so horny."

You spring up and pull on Rich's hair. He removes his mouth from me and I sigh because it felt so good.

"Kneel up baby," you urge me and I do as I'm told, kneeling on the bed on all fours.

Kneeling in front of me on the bed, you offer me your rock hard cock and I smile at you, teasing the head with my tongue, lapping over the top and rolling around the tip, sucking you in a little bit and then releasing, then working my tongue down your shaft and back to the tip again. I groan against your cock as I feel Rich's tongue on my arse, lapping and probing my hole, his fingers inside my pussy which is dripping so much right now it must be down his arm.

I suck your cock harder and harder, deep into my mouth, and you hold onto my head and thrust gently into my waiting lips.

"Stick your cock in her," I hear you say to Rich and I tense a little because your mate is about to fuck me, but you stroke my hair.

"It's okay baby, I want him to fuck you. I want you to enjoy his rock hard cock as you suck on mine."

Rich slaps my arse playfully and I groan against your cock as he slides into my waiting pussy, all the way in, deep and hard. He's so big and it fills me completely. I expect you can feel the vibrations through your cock and balls as I groan with each of his thrusts.

He starts slowly and he's so good, twisting his body to rub against my clit as he fucks me. I can hardly concentrate on sucking your cock, but I do the best I can. I can't believe how horny it feels to have two men filling me up so deliciously.

I'm such a little whore right now, your little whore.

You start to push your cock harder into my mouth as Rich starts to fuck me with the same intensity. I feel your body tense, are you straining your neck to watch him sliding into my pussy? I know you are because your cock gets even harder as it rams into my mouth, causing me to almost choke on it.

Rich feels so good and I try to hold back but I can't. I start to moan louder with each thrust, my noises stifled around your straining cock and when he grabs my hips and pulls me back really hard, banging his balls against my clit. I explode, screaming on your cock, and you pull out quickly because it looks like you're about to cum and you must want to stop it. You grab the base of your cock, until your breath slows down, and I let out the full force of my scream as Richard brings me to a climax that has me collapsing on the bed because my limbs give way.

Rich pulls out and I catch my breath for a moment as I feel you stroking my back, walking around the edge of the bed. I can hear you and Rich talking but I have no idea what you're saying. I close my eyes for a second and relax and it's you I feel climb on top of me because you're lighter than Rich. You push open my legs and nestle your hips between them and I feel your cock at the entrance to my cunt and then pushing inside me. I sigh as you lay with your whole body on top of mine, pushing deep inside, your lips against my ear. "How did it feel to have his huge thick cock inside you," you ask as you gently fuck me. "Was he good?"

And I nod because it feels so good to have you inside me I can hardly talk.

"Tell me how good it felt."

"It felt so fucking good baby, his cock is huge and he made me cum so hard, thank you baby, thank you."

You bite my neck as you continue to fuck me slowly and then I feel fingers pushing underneath me and then against the front of my pussy, rubbing my clit, but it's not your fingers because they're in my hair, it must be Rich's hand.

I look behind me and notice him wanking his magnificent cock over the pair of us as he watches you fuck me slow and steady, your body hard against mine your cock deep inside my pussy.

"I want to suck his cock while you fuck me," I say, and you grin as you lean in and kiss me.

You pull out and roll off me and I pin you down on the bed and climb on top of you in reverse cowgirl, sliding down your cock and rubbing my pussy against your balls. Rich climbs onto the bed and stands in front of me, his cock springing from his body, and I have to grab it to keep it still so I can suck on it.

I time my thrusts on your cock with my slurps on his, rising up off you and taking him all into my mouth and lowering myself onto you and licking his head. I start slowly but the feeling of both of you fucking me is amazing and soon I'm rising and falling on your cock fast and hard and struggling to contain Rich's cock in my mouth as I bounce on you, choosing to wank it into my mouth and suck the head to keep up a good pace.

"That's it wank that fucking cock," you shout at me. "Take that whole thing in your mouth and suck it baby, I want to see you suck his cock until his balls nearly explode."

Rich laughs as he grabs the back of my head and gently forces his cock further into my mouth and I gag a little because I'm still trying to fuck you as well, but I manage to keep a consistent movement despite the difficulty.

Rich starts to moan as I suck him deep and I can hear your breath has increased and you're now arching to fuck me harder and harder but you stop all of a sudden.

"I want Rich to fuck your arse," you say and I pull back from Rich's cock confused for a minute.

"But I want you to fuck me baby," I winge and you smile at me. "I'm going to be fucking you, don't you worry about it."

Rich climbs off the bed and you lay me on my side positioning yourself facing me, your hands tight on my back and your eyes with mine. You kiss me as you slide into my pussy which slurps around your cock because it's so wet. I lean into your shoulder as you start to fuck me, a crazy grin on your face.

I can't see Rich but I hear the lid of the lube and then feel the cold wet jelly against my arse as Rich fingers probe and then push inside me, stretching me out, and even that feels amazing with your cock inside me and his fingers up my arse.

I gasp. "Fuck that's good."

"You wait 'till his dicks up there," You whisper and then kiss me as I feel Rich lay down, tangling his limbs with yours and mine and pressing his cock against my arse. I'm scared for a minute because he's so huge and I've never been fucked up the arse with a cock that big before, but he's stretched me out good. Still, it hurts like hell as he slides into me, both my pussy and arse completely stretched to bursting with the pressure from both of your cocks, and I almost pass out, my head back against Rich's chest as he holds around my neck. I bet that feels amazing for you, to feel Rich's cock against your own as you both penetrate me so fully.

I can barely breathe as you both start to fuck me, careful to build up your speed gradually so you keep in time with each other, thrusting up inside me, filling me up so beautifully. Two glorious rock hard cocks pumping in and out of my holes. I grab hold of your chest, my head tight against Rich's and I'm aware that I'm screaming now because the pleasure is too much for me to handle.

"You love having two fucking hard cocks up you, don't you?" you ask me, and I scream my reply "Fuck yes, yes, yes, fuck you're gonna make me cum so hard."

Rich cums first, grabbing hold of my neck as his cock rams into my arse and I feel his spunk shooting up inside me and squirting back out again as he withdraws with a loud grunt and shoots more spunk over my arse cheeks, and as he does I cum, clamping around your cock, my orgasm so intense my arms and legs shudder, and I make a sound like an animal in pain.

You grab around my arse your hands slipping in his spunk and start to fuck me so hard I hardly have time to breath, your rock hard cock pounding every inch of my pussy. You've got a crazy horny look in your eyes and I feel you tense completely. I dig my nails into your arse and you cum deep inside me, letting out a groan as you do. I can feel your spunk hitting the walls of my pussy and every part of you is rigid as your cock keeps pumping inside me and then you relax your grip, your breath slowing.

I smile as you pull out because that's all I can do, totally spent from exhaustion and the intensity of the orgasm I just had. I feel you

30

slide down my body and smile as you lap at my arse, licking up the spunk and when Rich joins you to clean out my pussy I close my eyes and sigh.

The Flicks

An icy wind blows through my coat and I shiver against it. The sun is high in the sky but it does nothing to heat the November day, and my heels clip against the pavement as I hurry my way towards the cinema.

It took me ages to find somewhere to park and even longer debating if I really should take off my dress and bra and walk half way across town with just knickers and stockings on under my coat. My nipples rub against the satin lining as I increase my stride glancing down at my watch. I'm going to be late.

I round the corner, startled when I don't see you. Picking up speed I sprint across the cobbles until I reach the booking office and brush down my hair as I catch my breath. The geek behind the counter pushes up his glasses and smiles wide at me. "I was starting to get worried you wouldn't show."

I scowl at him, raising my hands in a question.

He dangles a ticket between his fingers, wiping his nose on his hand and fidgeting in his seat as he looks me up and down. "He told me you'd flash me for your ticket."

I scoff. "Like fuck he did."

The geek nods as if he expected that response, before reaching in front of him and pushing a piece of paper at me. I pick it up and open it.

`Flash for your ticket.`

I smirk as I read the words, there's no mistaking your handwriting. Are you watching me from somewhere inside? Are you stroking your cock while you wait for me to flash this guy, but really flash you?

The geek grins as I grab the belt of my coat and slide it open, pulling at the buttons until they're all undone. My throat dries and I have trouble swallowing as I check no-one else is around, and then flash him. I should be appalled at what I'm doing, exposing myself to a complete stranger at your request, but I'm not, not in the slightest. Knowing that I'm really doing it for you me makes it feel so horny my pussy drips in excitement and I have to stop my fingers wandering into my underwear right in the middle of the street.

I think the geek might cum in his trousers, his hands start shaking and he loses his glasses in his haste to lean forward and check out what he obviously couldn't see from the seat.

33

"So can I have my ticket now?" I shudder as my skin gooses and my nipples are painful as the cold bites them to attention. I close my coat around me as my cheeks flush scarlet with warmth.

I hope you enjoyed the show.

The geek disappears before coming back up with his glasses, reaching out for the piece of paper still in my hand. He grabs a pen scribbles something on it and hands it back to me with the ticket. I can see his rock hard cock straining against his trousers and I smile at him as I sashay away, the thrill of what I just did causing my heart to hammer in my chest loud enough to hear.

I'm directed to screen three and as I push through the heavy burgundy doors my legs start to tremble and I feel my pussy soak with juice. I smile as I notice you, but you're sitting in the middle of the room rather than the back like we'd agreed. How on earth are we going to get away with it there, what were you thinking?

The moth eaten seats and sticky floor make this place feel so decidedly seedy that I can't help giggling, how on earth do you talk me into these things? A faint trace of bleach reaches my nostrils as I make it to the aisle you're sat in and sneak between the seats towards you. You don't turn your head but you must know it's me because a tiny smile spreads across your lips, you swallow hard, and I notice you tense in the chair. Are you as excited as I am right now?

I sit next to you and you still don't turn, but I feel your hand in mine and you squeeze it, before removing the piece of paper the geek gave me and reading the message. A wry smile spreads across your face as you tuck the piece of paper in your shirt. I really should have checked what he wrote on that.

I smile as I settle in my seat, letting my legs fall open slightly as I do. As my coat's unbuttoned it parts to reveal my thighs. I grin as you sneak a glance at the tops of my stockings. Are you frustrated you can't see my panties and suspenders? I undo the belt of my coat and pull the front apart, just enough for you to see how tight my knickers are against the lips of my pussy, but keeping my tits hidden, to torment you.

I grin as I eye the huge bulge in your trousers and can't resist reaching out and rubbing my wrist against it as I undo your fly. You jump when I manage to free your cock, glancing about nervously. You're the one who sat in the middle of the theatre, not me. I follow your gaze, there's only a handful of people aside from us and they're more concerned with their snacks right now. I feel you relax as your

34

eyes meet mine but your breath is ragged as you lean in to kiss me. It feels electric, and I hardly notice when the trailers start, because your fingers are running up my thigh and then in my knickers, teasing the entrance to my pussy. Can you feel how wet I am?

You graze my clit with your fingertip as I slowly wank your cock, and the danger of doing this in a public place seems to triple the excitement. I can't stop grinning and neither can you, and when you pull open my coat with your other hand and lean into me, taking a nipple in your mouth, I gasp and grab a chunk of your hair.

You twist your body so you can push your fingers inside me, and you lean in so we can kiss again, your fingers deep in my pussy and your thumb working my clit. I'm vaguely aware the trailers are still on but I can't concentrate on anything other than the pleasure you're delivering me right now.

You move your hand curling your fingers until you find my g-spot. I pull back from your lips and shake my head, if you make me cum like that I'll gush all over the seat, but you don't stop, pressing my g and rubbing my clit insistently. Fuck - that is insanely good. My breath is heaving now. I've slid so far down the seat my knees are pressing into the back of the chair in front but it gives me leverage to push against your hand and it will only take a minute to cum like this.

I can't keep hold of your cock as you lean in to suck my nipple, so I grip the arms of the seat as you work your lips up to my mouth, and you kiss me to stifle my cry as I cum, my thighs gripping your hand and forearm, and elbowing you in the chest as my whole body convulses.

You pull your hand away and cum soaks my panties, the back of my coat and I'm sure the seat beneath me. I sit still for a moment to catch my breath, completely dazed by the intensity, and you grin at me the way you always do when you make me cum that hard. Fuck, you're amazing.

I lean in and kiss you, clawing at your neck and hair, my orgasm only serving to make me hornier for you. I smile as I reach for your cock, still nice and hard for me. Taking it in my hand, I start to wank you slowly again, tugging at your jeans slightly so I can reach in and massage your balls.

I'm startled by a noise but it's just the curtains opening further. The movies about to start but I don't think we'll be watching much of it. I smile as the lights start to dim, knowing that this is your favourite part.

Would you like to feel my mouth on your cock right now?

As the room descends to darkness and everyone else is lost in the movie, I know you're lost to the feel of my hot lips as I surround your shaft, my tongue toying with the tip, flicking hard against it then softly lapping, flicking hard again then sucking you in a little so you can feel my mouth around your head, hot and tight, surrounding you in warmth. How does it feel to have me sucking your cock right in the middle of the cinema?

I can't even describe how hot this makes me. I slurp your cock into my mouth and I feel your hand on my shoulder as I take you deep. I'm sure I hear you groaning even over the movie, fuck you must be really enjoying this.

I keep lapping the pre-cum from your head, revelling in your delicious taste and scent as my head's buried in your lap, trying to block out the sounds of gun fire and shouting coming from the screen. I want you to spunk deep in my throat, I want to make you cum so much right now that I start to bob harder and faster and use my hands as well, but you must have other ideas about where you want to cum, because you grab the back of my hair sharply and stop me moving. I keep my head still but I don't rest up, using my tongue and swallowing against your cock until you pull my hair gently so your cock falls free of my mouth and you keep pulling me up until you're looking into my eyes. Do you want to spunk on my tits?

"Sit on my cock," you mouth at me.

"Are you crazy? We're in the middle of the cinema, giving you a blow job is one thing but fucking is going to be impossible in here, someone will notice that."

You shrug. "So."

Really? You really want to fuck me right now?

I giggle as I look about. There's only one couple behind us to the far right, they look pretty engrossed in the film. They will be able to see us fucking from where they're sitting if they look over, but I'm so crazy horny right now I'm beyond caring, and how can I turn you down, I can never turn you down and you know it.

You sit up in the seat as you pull me onto your lap. I arch up on tiptoes and you push my soaking underwear to one side as you slide your cock into me.

"Fuck, fuck, fuck, fuck," I mutter as I lean my head onto the seat in front, sure that if anyone sees my face they'll know for sure that you're pounding the hell out of me right now because my grin is from ear to ear and my face is poker hot.

You slide down in your seat so you can use the one in front for leverage to push up into me, and grab my hips as you start to move a little faster and harder. Your cock stretching me with every thrust, filling me up completely, your fingers digging into my hips, and the plastic of the seat in front freezing against my tits as your hip movements push me into it.

You buck up harder, fuck that feels so good. I want to cry out with every movement you make and I have to bite my arm to stop myself. One of your hands leaves my hips and I feel it push between me and the seat as you grab me round the tits and shoulder, and push even deeper into my pussy. You sit up to change angle, I grip the seat in front but have to lean my head back against your shoulder so I don't bang my head, hooking my feet under the seat so I can add some resistance for you to work with.

It causes you to fuck me even harder and I can't stop myself from crying out.

You clamp your hand over my mouth. "Shush for fucks sake," you hiss in my ear, but then you whisper. "How much are you enjoying this right now? How do you like me fucking the hell out of your cunt like this?"

I love it when you fuck me with your words as well as your cock, when I hear the sound of your voice in my ears so it feels like your fucking my mind as well as my body.

"I love it." I answer.

"Tell me how much you love it," you demand.

"A lot."

You push harder and faster and I know you're as close as I am because your breath is deafening in my ears and your grip around my tits is so tight it's painful.

"Tell me how much you love it," you growl, as your arm slips up around my neck.

"Fuck, I love it so much. I don't ever want it to stop."

Your arm cuts off my breath with every stroke but only enough to increase the pleasure.

"Oh my God I'm gonna cum." I'm sure I just yelled that, but I don't give a shit because I'm cumming so hard on your cock right now I have to use all my concentration to keep moving so you can cum too, and when I hear your long low groan in my ear and feel your cock jump and your cum flooding me, I know you came as hard as I did. I turn my head and kiss the side of your face, toying with the hair at the base of your neck as we relax and our breath slows to normal.

You glance about as I do. No-one looks even remotely aware of what we were just doing in here, not even the couple behind us. We both laugh as we kiss again. I can't believe we had the nerve to go through with it.

My legs are killing me as I climb off and flop back into my own seat, taking a long draw of cola. My knickers are soaked but it doesn't bother me, it just reminds me of how much fun we just had.

"I have no idea what's going on," you smirk as you point to the screen.

"Me neither," I whisper in your ear. "I don't think it matters really, what we were doing was far more interesting." I shiver as I take another draw of cola.

"You're freezing," you say looking concerned.

I nod because I am all of a sudden.

"Come on let's go, we got what we came for," you smirk and grab my hand, pulling me towards the end of the aisle.

It's startlingly bright outside as we leave the cinema. Your grin is as wide as mine as you push me against the wall and steal a kiss. As you're pulling away I notice the piece of paper in the pocket of your shirt, and before you can stop me I pull it out and read it.

`Make her gush all over the seat so I can sniff it later.`

"Dirty bastard," I giggle. I grip around your neck and you look confused as I pull down my knickers, step out of them, and hand them to you.

"Really?" you ask me.

I nod, and you shrug, a bounce in your step as you walk to the counter.

The fantastic fucking you just gave me, and the look on the geek's face when you hand him my cum soaked knickers, is going to be more than enough to make up for the freezing walk back to the car, and I know you'll have plenty of suggestions for warming me back up when we get there.

Make me beg

I lean back against your chest, the hot water lapping my nipples. You rub my arm with your fingers, chewing my ear gently, and I nuzzle back towards you with a sigh.

Work was shit, traffic was even shitter, and I was ready to flop into bed after a ready meal, but when I got home and you'd poured me a glass of red, run a bath, and promised to make me forget all about it, I did, in an instant. How do you always do that? Know just what I need and when I need it.

"Feeling better?" you ask me and I smile as I nod, taking the last sip of wine to drain the glass. You reach for the bottle but I shake my head, I'm feeling pretty drunk right now already and I don't want to fall asleep on you.

I turn to put my glass on the side and you steal a kiss, your lips soft against mine, your tongue probing my mouth and then moving in tandem with me. I close my eyes, feel your stubble scratching the side of my face, and breathe in the scent of the bath oil, combined with feint traces of your aftershave.

"Where did you go?" you ask me, and I snap out of my daze.

"Just relaxing."

"Good," you smile and run your hands down to my nipples, rubbing them gently with the palms, as you massage my breasts.

"Oh, so you had an ulterior motive for this bath then?" I ask, arching my brow, and you grin. That fucking crazy horny grin you have that makes my insides melt.

"Would I do that…"

I lean in and cut you off with a kiss, my tongue desperate to search out all of your mouth and my hands hard on your neck to pull you into me as close as I can get you.

You push back gently. "You sounded pretty tense when you called me from the car. A tense you equals an unhappy you, I just figured you might need some help with that."

I bite my lip as your hands snake their way down my body, resting against my mound. I clench with need, heat flooding my insides.

"So… what are you… going to do to help me?" I ask you, breathing hard.

You push a finger over the edge and nudge it against my clit. "I thought I might start here," you breathe against my neck. "Thought I might rub that clit of yours between my fingers just like this."

You know I love it when you talk dirty to me. Your soft deep voice resonating inside my head gets me wet in seconds. Hell, I'm already wet just thinking about it.

"mmmm," I mumble.

"Move my finger like this."

I suck air in as you flick my clit gently.

"Maybe stick my fingers in your tight little pussy like this."

I arch back as you press your fingers inside me, twisting your body slightly so you can push them in fully, rubbing your thumb against my clit.

"Is that helping?" you ask, right in my ear.

I nod, but can't speak.

I keep my eyes closed to focus on the pleasure you're giving me, breathing hard as you send my body into overdrive, every tiny nerve to attention, a deep longing inside me that you satisfy so well.

"Do you like it when I rub your cunt like this," you ask me, and I jolt as your lips brush my ear and your sexy voice grates against it.

"Uh-huh," I approve.

"How about when I twist my fingers like this?"

The noise I make is incomprehensible as a word but I know you'll understand. You twist your fingers again, applying more pressure to my clit, the lapping hot water heightening the thrill.

I grip hold of your thighs, my head tipping back against you. Your movements quicken and cause the water to splash. I hear it slapping the side of the tub. Your free hand moves to my forehead, turning my head to the side. Is that so you can watch yourself finger my pussy, or watch the pleasure on my face as you make me cum?

My legs are so tense they're in pain. I push against the end of the bath to allow you to dip your fingers further inside me, your hand slapping the water now with each thrust. You're rock hard, your balls against my arse and your cock straining against my back.

I feel my orgasm starting, a little ripple at first, travelling with speed, and then increasing in intensity as you continue to move your fingers. I can't help thrusting myself against your hand. You must be able to tell I'm about to cum. You kiss me, running your tongue over my lips, and my pussy tightens, my thighs tighten, everything tightens, before it's released. I buckle against you surprised by its strength, and you keep your fingers still as the sensations wash over me, and until they subside.

I open my eyes. You were watching my face when I came, I can tell. You've often told me you love to watch my face as I cum, that it's the best thing on this earth to know that you caused that kind of pleasure, that you made me feel that good.

You remove your fingers and relax your hand against the top of my thigh, the other pushing back hair that's stuck to my face.

"I think that might have done the trick," you smirk.

"For starters," I smile back.

I sit up and swivel round so I'm facing you, water splashing over the edge of the bathtub as I do. Reaching out with my toes I rub them against your balls. You roll your head back and groan at me. You're so hard. I continue to massage your balls with my toes before I take your shaft between both feet and start to move slowly up and down. The hot water swirls around the base of your cock, but the tip breeches the surface. The air must be cooling it as it does. I wonder what that feels like for you?

You cover your eyes and groan again. I giggle because I know I'm moving too slowly to do anything but drive you to distraction, but I also know you love it. When you groan again, this time with more force, I know it's time to stop teasing you.

You roll your eyes now. "Please," you whisper.

I smile as I push up onto all fours and lick the tip of your cock. It springs away from me in excitement so I have to grab it to keep it still. I take you into my mouth, just a fraction, run my tongue in swirls around the top, gently massage with my hot wet lips. I submerge my mouth and suck in water before spitting it back over your head and then drawing in a breath to cool it. You shudder against me. I do the same again and you shudder, harder this time.

I feel your hips lifting up. I bet you're desperate just to fuck my mouth right now? I lower my head slowly so I can take you all in without gagging, and your hands move to my shoulders as you sigh. I suck deep and hard, using my tongue on the underside to apply pressure and swallowing occasionally to give you a different sensation.

You start to moan softly, each breath coming faster than the last and your hands tightening their grip and moving to the back of my neck. I work with the slight thrusts of your hips to give you the speed you need, but I'm surprised when you pull up my head.

"It's no good, I need to fuck you," you pant.

I smile, moving myself to straddle you but you shake your head and push up.

41

"What…"

I squeal as you pick me up and climb out of the bath with me. We're dripping wet but you don't even grab any towels, just carry me into the bedroom and throw me down on the bed.

"We're all wet…"

You give me your serious face, the one that tells me I'm being a bore, and I know I'm for it now because you glower at me. You're rough as you flip me over and push me up the bed. You must be really horny right now. I wonder if you're just going to slide your cock into me, but you reach for the leather handcuffs we keep attached to the bed, and secure one wrist before I have a chance to wiggle out of your grip.

You sit on my back so I can't get up, but I've stopped fighting you anyway. I relax my arm so you can put it in the other restraint, and you pull hard to make sure it's secure. Reaching back to the chair by the window, you grab the scarf I was wearing to work. My heart's pounding as you tie it around my head, depriving me of light, but heightening my other sensations.

How do I look right now, my body still wet from the bath, trembling with cold, fear and excitement? My cunt swells and starts dripping.

You brush your fingers through my hair, and I feel the bed depress as you climb on in front of me. Your cock knocks against my chin, and I open my mouth instinctively to suck you. I feel your hand against my face as you guide your cock into my waiting lips. You groan as I start to lick your head. I'm surprised when you don't shove your cock down my throat. I'm all bound up with no-where to go, what's stopping you? I push forward to take more of you in and you groan out your appreciation your hand moving to the back of my head. I'm not really at the best angle to take you in fully, so I carefully move my legs forward so I'm kneeling, and I feel you push up your hips to aid me further.

Now I can suck you in deep and hard, and I slurp on your cock, working furiously on the shaft and licking the head when I reach I pull you out of my mouth.

Mmmmmm, I mumble against you. Does that send vibrations up your cock and through your balls? You certainly like it because you pound into my throat and cause me to choke a little.

"Sorry babes," you stroke my cheek, before pulling out of me.

Where are you going? I haven't finished sucking your cock yet. I want to finish sucking you off.

I turn my head, frustrated I can't see you right now. I stop moving and listen intently. I can hear you breathing close to my ear. You run your hands down my back and I arch because it tickles. I know you're smirking at me, even if I can't see you. You tickle me again and I arch harder, throwing back my head. This time you laugh.

I feel you grab my behind and pull me up so I'm on all fours again, are you kneeling down behind me? You take a cheek into your mouth and bite gently and I sigh as you nibble on my flesh. Then I feel your fingers against my pussy, wiping some of my juice with them. Are you licking your fingers now? I feel you breathe against my slick wet hole and I clench in anticipation. You leave me waiting, and I huff impatiently. Dipping your finger just inside me your tongue makes me jump as you lick my arse, bringing a flood of heat that flows through my body as my arousal increases.

Your fingers plunge deep inside me and I know I must be covering you with my sweetness because I'm so horny. I feel the bed depress again, you must have climbed back on. I can't contain my excitement, and I feel fluttering in my stomach as you rub the head of your cock against my tight wet pussy. I want you inside me so badly I can't think of anything else.

Do you love to have me as your fuck toy?

You push into me slowly. You bastard. I need to fuck me hard right now and you know it. You're torturing me for your own amusement. You move gently back and forwards, running your hands over my arse. You're watching yourself fuck me, I know it, watching your cock pushing deep inside me and then pulling out, watching every torturous, excruciating thrust. You continue for a couple of minutes, holding my hips hard so I have no way of pushing back onto you, then you pull out completely and push me gently, signalling me to roll over. I have to twist my arms as I'm still restrained but I manage it, lying back on the bed and letting my legs fall apart.

Are you gazing at my pussy right now? Can you see how wet I am for you, how horny you're making me? I feel your cock against my thigh. I smile. I know you're just as horny as I am. You love it when I'm bound like this, completely at your mercy, when I submit and trust you completely.

I pull on the restraints because I long to hold your cock in my hands, but I feel it nudge my clit and slide its way down to the

43

entrance of my pussy. I arch back, my whole body tingling with excitement. You push into me and I'm in heaven as you fill me with your hard cock and lay down on top of me.

Your hands are in my hair and on my face as you kiss my lips and our tongues dance. All the while you move slowly, teasingly, you want this to last as long as I do, but it's so damn horny and your cock feels so good I can hardly control myself.

"Please," I beg.

"Please, what?" you whisper in my ears.

"Please fuck me faster, harder."

"No," you reply.

Do you love it when I beg you, when you make me so horny I make a sound in the back of my throat like an animal? I know you do because your cock stiffens even more than I thought was possible.

You increase your pace enough to tease me even more, but not enough to satisfy me completely. I know you're loving this right now, feeling my hips writhe beneath you, arching up greedily so your body rubs against my clit. I moan as you grip my nipple between your teeth.

I pull against my restraints. "You need to untie me now," I demand, and you laugh at me again.

"I don't."

"You do, you need to let me out right now."

"What you going to do if I don't?" you ask, and stop moving.

I arch up even harder, clenching my hands into fists, my nails digging in as I do. I feel tears of frustration sting my eyes underneath the blindfold. "Please, please just fuck me harder, I need it, I want it so badly, please."
I hate to have to beg you to fuck me, but I can't help myself. You get me so wet, crazy and horny.

You pull off the blindfold and I have to squint for a moment until my eyes focus. You're smile is wide as you brush a tear from my eye. You lean on an elbow and undo one arm, before reaching over and untying the other.

Kissing me, with your elbows either side of my head, you push deep inside, filling me with every inch of you until I gasp. I grip around your waist with my thighs, my hands tight on your back, my nails clawing at your skin, but you don't move, you only smile at me. I kick my heels into your butt but you still don't move. Fuck, what are you doing to me?

"God, I need you to fuck me, please, please…"

"On top?" you ask.

I nod eagerly, and you pull out and roll over.

I feel so empty without you in my dripping cunt. I push up quickly, straddling your stomach. I rub against you, bathing you in juice. Now it's you that arches up against me. I smile. I thought as much, all the while teasing me mercilessly when you're just as horny as I am.

I torment the head of your cock with my pussy, and you growl as you grab my hips and pull me onto you with force. I bite my lip and my head falls back at the feel of your glorious cock deep inside me. I want to tease you but it's impossible because I need to fuck the hell out of you, right now.

I move my hips rocking back and forwards and up and down in tandem and you hold me tightly, pushing up to meet my thrusts. Our bodies start to sweat. I grind into you with as much force as I can and you match me. Do you want to cum as much as I do right now? Is every muscle in your body aching from exhaustion, but driving you to work harder and faster against me?

You move your hands onto my arse and I know you're close because of that sexy sound you make. I change angle to rub my clit against you, but I need more, and you understand because you sit up, holding me to your chest so I can rub against your body.

I ride you with everything I have in me, our bodies tight and hot together. I can barely drag in enough breath to keep conscious, and as I move I feel my release, that beautiful moment just before I cum when I know nothing in the world will stop it. I concentrate hard on how much you fill me, on how good your body feels against mine, on how amazing you are, and then I cum so hard I bite into your shoulder.

You let out a groan and push up against me.

"Let go baby," I whisper. "I want you to fill me with your hot spunk right now."

You arch a little and I pinch your nipples hard as you cum. I feel your cock twitching within my tight hole, filling me up with your cream. I wonder what it feels like for you when you spunk up inside me? To feel my pussy gripping you hard as your cock fights against it, pulsing as more and more of your cum fills me up to bursting. To me if feels like the best thing in the world.

You smile and kiss me before falling back on the bed, and I climb off. Lying down next to you I smile, basking in the feel of your

45

cum trickling down my arse crack and my pussy lips still quivering with pleasure.

The velvet room

It's quiet when we enter the red velvet room, just a single girl in a G-string lounging back on a chaise. I nod at her, and she smiles with an arched eyebrow, her eyes showing just a hint of hunger. You sit on the edge of the daybed and smile at me as I linger in the doorway, snaking my body up and down the frame in a seductive dance, the thud of the base line from the club below my guiding rhythm. I watch with interest as the bulge in your suit pants increases in size.

I turn my back on you and slide my dress off, shaking my arse. Do you like my lace French knickers and the stockings I wore for you? I unhook my bra, turning back over my shoulder and biting my lip, before dropping it to the floor. You remove your tie, teasingly, slowly, throwing it to join my dress, and my heart skips a little.

I turn back to you, my breasts hidden behind my hands, and giggle. You wink at me as you remove your jacket, slip off your shoes and socks, and start to unbutton your shirt. I feel my breath quicken, and my pulse nudges up as you slide it off revealing your glorious body to me.

Chaise girl sits up, her keen interest indicated by the way she's clenching her legs together and licking her lips.

I remove my hands from my breasts and walk towards you, turning as I reach you and brushing my arse against your knees, sliding them up your legs to settle on your still covered cock. You lean in against my back, your lips and tongue leaving a trail of shivers behind them as you lick me. Working your way up to my neck, you bite gently before doing the same on my ear. I sigh as my head falls back against your shoulder. Your hands brush my thighs, sneaking around the top of my stockings, then just inside them, across my waist and up my back. I arch against you again, this time my sigh is louder, and I turn as you put your lips on mine and kiss me, slow and deep, your hand in my hair.

I get up and sit back on your lap facing you. You brush a strand of hair away before you kiss me again, this time with more force and urgency as I press my tits into your chest. I notice you glancing at Chaise girl and feel your cock grow beneath me. Does it turn you on even more because we're being watched right now by a pretty blonde in a tiny thong, barely a foot away from us? I know it does, and it makes me drip at the thought of it.

I kiss you again, feeling your hands on my back and then my buttocks, massaging them beneath your fingers. I grind myself against you, thinking of how I'm going to be fucking you soon. How I'm going to feel that thick cock deep inside, filling me up so completely, while the pretty blonde looks on longingly.

I undo your belt and slide it out before reaching down and unzipping your fly, brushing my hand inside. You grin at me. Is your heart racing as much as mine? I know it is when I put my hand against your chest and feel it thumping.

Pushing me off, you stand and remove your trousers and boxers as I lay back on the daybed and admire you in all your splendour. You look magnificent in the dim light from the hallway outside, every muscle in your body tense, your glorious cock rock hard for me.

I catch myself sighing again.

I lift up my bum as you remove my knickers, sliding them slowly off the edge of my toes , bringing your lips down against my calves and ankles, and working your way up my stockings, across my hips, up my torso and then to my nipple, which you suck lazily into your mouth and flick with your tongue.

I notice the blonde's hands tense a little.

You nestle beside me and we tangle our limbs as we kiss. There's no rush, we like to take our time when we're watched, give the audience a great show. My hands wander the length of your torso, your arms, back and face, and you pull on my nipples as you kiss my neck.

I'm already soaking, even before your fingers find my clit and rub it with long slow strokes. I make a sound at the back of my throat as I close my eyes. I concentrate on the feel of your hands on me, working me with a skill only you possess. I hear the sounds of whispering, someone else must have joined the blonde, perhaps a couple, perhaps even more, because I hear multiple hushed voices now.

I feel myself flood with juice and you lean into my ear and whisper, "You're so wet tonight. You love it when we're being watched. There's five people in here now, watching my fingers rubbing your clit and now," you push inside me as I arch against you, "deep inside your pussy."

And I nod, biting down on my palm as I let out a low moan of approval.

48

You know exactly what to do to me, and I can only lay there and enjoy the feel of your fingers inside me, your mouth against my own, and your tongue fighting with mine. Pushing your fingers deeper and using your thumb and palm against my clit pushes me over the edge. I grab around your head with both arms, my elbows tight on your shoulders. You lean into me, is it so you can hear me urging you on as I mutter, "Fuck that's so good. God... please don't stop...please..." I feel my legs tense, my muscles in pain as my whole body tightens... and then releases. I grip you tightly and pant into your mouth as I cum, my pussy gripping your hand like a vice as I explode, and I don't release my grip until the sensations ease off.

You pull against my waist with your arm, and I roll on top of you, our bodies pressed tight together. I push myself off your chest and guide your cock into me. Groaning as you push in deep, and clamping my knees around your hips. You hold my tits as I ride you, rotating to bring my clit in contact with your body, and drive you in further. I can feel your thighs tight beneath me as my knees clamp around your body. You push up in small movements and I come down to meet you, every stroke bringing exquisite pleasure.

As you sit up you grip me to you, our mouths meeting again. Does that feel as good for you as it does for me? You hold my backside and I rock against you. Nothing rushed or frantic, just two people joined together, feeling everything as if in slow motion. You bring up your knees and I lean back against them so I can grind my body into yours and your head falls to my breasts, sucking one into your mouth. We can hardly move now but it doesn't matter, just the feel of our bodies together is enough, and we rock slowly.

You lower your legs again as I lean in and kiss you, our hands rough in each other's hair and starting to move faster and harder against each other. You grab my wrist and pull it behind my back, then the other, holding both of my arms pinned behind me with one hand, continuing to run your free one over my breasts and stomach. I struggle to free myself, wanting to touch you, but you don't let me. It only serves to heighten my thrill. I lean my head onto your shoulder, as you hold me captive, and gently bite it with each stroke of your cock.

You lift your head in a sharp nod, your signal that you want to change position. I climb off, and lean on all fours. You bite my arse gently before moving your tongue against my hole, reaching under and teasing my pussy with your fingers. I dip my shoulders lowering onto

49

my elbows as your tongue and fingers deliver me pleasure until I can barely stand it, lapping over my pussy and then back to my waiting arse.

My breath speeds up to a frantic pace, my hands clawing to grab hold of something, anything, but finding only each other, and I clasp them together in ecstasy, each breath now accompanied by a moan or a gasp. When I feel your wet thumb in my arse I know it's only going to be seconds before I cum again, and it is. You pull out your thumb hard, causing me to cum in a sharp spasm, clamping down on your hands and crushing your arm between my thighs. I don't even need to turn around to know your smiling. I know you love to make me cum so hard and fast.

Your hands are quickly on my waist and then your cock against my pussy. You push in, using my hips as leverage.

"Fuck," I yell at the intrusion, a mixture of pleasure and pain on top of the last threads of my orgasm.

You fuck me slowly, your hands on my back and shoulders and I look back and smile at you. Your eyes are closed as you move against me. You look like you are really enjoying yourself right now.

How does it feel to be in my tight hot pussy, fucking me like this while all these people watch us?

I feel your body tense and know you're close. You sigh as you pull out of me and I fall onto my side on the daybed. Your fingers snake up my back as you lay next to me, and I lean in grabbing you around the neck and kiss you. I feel your rock hard cock pressing against my stomach and think it's been seriously neglected by my mouth so far.

I tease my tongue down your torso. Reaching your cock, I lick the head in long laps, swirling my tongue around the tip, massaging it with my lips, before running my tongue down your whole shaft and licking your balls. You taste of me and you together, and it's delicious. I bite teasingly, sucking skin into my mouth and releasing you again. I suck your whole length in deep for a while using my tongue on the underside and swallowing against you every now and again. You smile as you stroke my hair and I look you in the eyes. I love watching your face as I suck your cock. Do you like watching me suck you?

I pull away from you and lay on the daybed with my head hanging off the edge. Your smile is wicked when you work out my plan.

The daybed's not high enough for you to stand so you kneel and I take your cock in my hand and guide it into my waiting lips. At this angle you can enter my throat fully and you fuck my mouth deep, but slowly so I can breathe. You hold the sides of my head with affection as you slide your cock in and out. I know it's taking every bit of your willpower not to push harder and faster but you know it'll choke me. I reach up and stroke your back before placing my hands on your balls and massaging gently. Blood rushes to my head and makes me dizzy, and I open my eyes slightly noticing all the people in the room have sat up and are watching with interest.

I feel your body tense again, this time sharply, and know you're very close but I also know you'll want to fuck me to oblivion in here. You pull out, your cock huge, and your balls swollen from the need to cum. I'm about to stand when I notice a couple lay on the floor, the other couple and the blonde joining them, beckoning with their hands. I give you a curious look and you shrug. I guess you're game if I am.

We've never fucked on a human carpet before, this should be fun.

Two sets of arms catch me as I lean back, positioning me directly over everyone's bodies so they can take the weight evenly. I feel hands on my skin, running down my sides, over my breasts, between my legs, but I have no idea who's touching me. It sends shivers down my spine, and the excitement in the room is tangible.

You watch for a moment. Is it exciting you to watch others touching me, knowing I have no idea whose hands are on me and what they'll do next? It must be because your cock looks about ready to explode right now.

It doesn't look easy for you to position yourself on top of everyone, we all giggle and manoeuvre until we're comfortable, and I start to have second thoughts about the practicalities of it, but when you push deep inside me, your eyes locked with mine, I've never been so excited in my life, and in an instant I forget everything.

Your elbows are either side of my head, resting on someone's stomach. I feel two rock hard cocks beneath me, one in the small of my back, and one by my neck. I can hear whispering, and the sounds of deep kisses. You don't close your eyes as you move inside me, deep and hard now, your speed increasing with every thrust. I desperately want to know what you can see, but you're so entranced I don't want

51

to distract you. I hear a whisper in my ear, soft and gentle, a woman's voice. Is it the g-string blonde?

She leans in kissing my neck, working her tongue against my ear before biting it. I feel a hand on my nipple, I wonder if that's her or someone else. I wish I could see myself right now like you can. Stranger's hands on my body and strangers voice in my ear. It's so exciting.

"Your man looks so fucking sexy right now, ploughing his cock into you. I bet he's having to hold back, grip his muscles tight to stop from cumming right this instant, watching me squeezing your nipples and now," I feel a hand on my chin and it turns my head to one side, "Kissing you."

Hot lips meet my own, soft and gentle, with a lazy tongue that darts into my mouth occasionally. I feel your body tense and your hands grab my hair. She pulls away but you dip your head into my shoulder and I hear her kissing you now. I open my eyes so I can see you both, and I feel my pussy spasm around your cock at the thrill of watching your lips against hers. Now there's a wet finger at my arse teasing me and I gasp as it pushes inside. Fuck that feels amazing, your thick cock inside me, a stranger's finger in my arse, while I watch you kiss the pretty blonde.

I feel a softer hand between my legs, nails scratching, reaching up for your balls no doubt, and you sigh, closing your eyes, leaning in to kiss me, the blondes tongue darting between us both. You increase your pace, a sharp moan escaping your mouth as you fuck me, leaning in to kiss the blonde again. I hold back as long as I can but your cock and the finger in my arse are too much, and when someone takes hold of a nipple and squeezes hard, I yell out, "Yes, oh God yes, fuck I'm gonna cum."

You lean into me, the whole force of your body causing you to ram me with your cock. "Hold on baby," you whisper.

I grab your backside digging my nails into it, and feel your back arch a little. I know you're about to cum and I want to hold it but I can't, because it feels so sublime and surreal to be fucking atop a writhing human bed.

You groan long and hard as you push with force and when I feel your cock jump inside me, I let go and join you. It feels amazing as my pussy clenches around your twitching cock, my juice combined with your cum, flooding me. Sweat drizzling down my breasts and stomach and onto those below us.

We're breathing hard for ages as we relax and kiss for a while. I feel the blonde roll out from beneath my head, and you hold me up as two more bodies slide out and then lower my back to the floor.

Climbing off me, your grin is huge. You bend down and pick me up as the last couple roll out. I have no idea how you're standing, as my legs and arms are totally numb. You lower me onto the day bed and lie next to me, and I rest my head against your chest, closing my eyes and listening to your heartbeat slow, and the sounds of fucking all around us, and I smile as I let out a contented purr.

Back to mine

You block my path in the doorway. Brushing my cheek as you push hair out of my face, and melting my insides with the look you give me. There's nothing but lust in your eyes and I guess as you're looking at me you'll know there's nothing but lust in mine either. You nudge me up against the door frame, and I can feel your confined rock hard cock pushing against my thigh as you dip your head and graze your lips against my ear. "Are you going to ask me in?"

I shudder as your breath hits my neck, your lips leaving a trail of wet behind as you kiss your way down to my shoulder, my resolve ebbing away with every single second. My tongue darts out my mouth, and my knees start to tremble as I feel your hand on the back of my thigh, sneaking up inside my skirt, higher up until you run it inside my lace knickers, circling your fingers on my arse cheek and then giving it a gentle squeeze.

I swallow hard, but my throat's still completely dry.

I tear my eyes from the vision of your cock straining against your jeans, and look deep into your eyes. You hold my stare unabashed, and in that very instant I'm yours. I have to have you. There's no way I can say no, not when you look at me like that, not when you give me a smile that could ignite my underwear, not when I sneak my fingers inside your t-shirt and feel your tight body.

"Are you going to ask me in?" Your voice has a tone of insistency that wasn't there before. I notice your breath has quickened and your pupils have dilated. I nod, because it's all I can do, and you let go of the handle allowing the door to swing open.

I can't get inside quick enough.

I'm unsteady in my heels, my heart almost beating out of my chest, my breath shallow and fast, my pussy so hot it feels like I've a poker between my legs, and when you push me up against the door as it closes, leaning in until your lips are a fraction from mine, until I can see nothing but your eyes and almost taste you, my legs give way.

You stop me from falling, holding around my back as your other hand slides around my neck, your lips closer than I thought possible without touching. I can feel your hot breath on my face as you turn your head slightly, and the anticipation of your kiss is almost too much.

You close your eyes as you narrow the gap to nothing, and your lips are warm as they touch mine, the faintest trace of wet on them. You're gentle, showing just the right amount of hunger without force, your tongue searching every inch of my mouth, dancing with mine, not fighting against it.

I feel my pussy contract, every nerve ending in my body on fire as your hands wander down to my breasts, tweaking a nipple through my top and bra until it's so hard it begs to be stripped bare and sucked into your mouth. I want to feel your hands and mouth on every bit of me, and I want to return the favour more than anything.

I lift my arms above my head as you remove my top, towering over me as you lean over my shoulder to undo my bra, casting it to the floor. Your hands on my skin cause me to shudder again, my breath increasing as you cup my breasts, tweaking my nipples into points, bending so you can suck one into your mouth as you start to undo my skirt, and I kick it off as it falls to the floor.

You kneel in front of me, kissing over my stomach as I plant my hands in your hair and tug gently, closing my eyes and leaning my head back against the door. Biting my lips harder as your tongue runs over my inner thighs in circles. I can feel your breath against my pussy and I grip your hair tighter. Are you breathing me in right now, teasing yourself with my scent before you take a taste?

I arch my back, pushing my hips into your face. I want you to feel your lips and tongue on me more than I think possible. I can't concentrate on anything but the heat spreading between my legs, causing me to breathe harder and faster, my limbs aching from arching into you, my hands gripping your hair tighter.

You look up at me. I can tell your chest is rising and falling fast as you hook your thumbs into my underwear and begin tugging until it's at my ankles, grinning as you stare at my pussy. I can't believe I'm naked apart from my heels and you're still fully clothed, how the hell did that happen, and in my hallway as well?

You kiss up the front of my thigh from my knee, ducking in-between my legs, teasing me with breath against my pussy, but nothing more, just breathing against me in rhythmic hypnotism. I arch from the door, and shudder when I feel the very tip of your tongue against me, sucking in air and gasping as you swirl over my clit.

Oh God that feels amazing.

I can barely keep balance in my heels, placing a hand on your shoulder to steady myself, leaning off the door so only my head is against it, to grind into your face. You hook your hands around my legs and pull me to your mouth.

56

I can't even comprehend what you are doing with your tongue. I've never felt anything like it before. So much pleasure it's almost too intense, sliding, sucking and biting over my clit, dipping into my pussy lips, then teasing the outside, tilting your head and licking me harder.

Your hands grip tight around my thighs nearly lifting me off the floor, and you seem frustrated. I lift my leg up over your shoulder, perhaps you need better access? You nod your approval as you push your tongue deep inside me.

"Oh fuck!" I whisper, my heel digging into your t-shirt and back until I'm worried I might rip it or hurt you, but you don't stop. You lick my clit again, this time bringing your fingers up and teasing the entrance to my pussy. The need inside me is at boiling point. I'm desperate for you to ram me with your whole hand right now but you take your time with slow steady movements, toying me with your fingers and tongue, bringing me so close it's almost unbearable.

I arch back, my forehead now against the door, and it only takes one of your fingers , gently pushed inside, to start the ripple. It's like pin pricks bursting out of my skin, and I release everything that you've built up in me, in a yell that both startles and thrills at the same time. I've never felt so good. Endorphins flood every cell of my body, warmth rising from my core and flushing all the way up to my face with scorching heat.

My smile's wide enough to hurt as the pleasure peaks and starts tumbling down again, my limbs shaking and my breath dragged in gasps as I just keep cumming and cumming, your tongue continually moving to prolong my orgasm, insistently. I tremble against your mouth, my thigh gripping your shoulder to try and stay upright, but I struggle and slump down the door as you emerge from between my legs, smiling wryly, your lips and chin glistening with cum. I have an irresistible urge to kiss you.

I crouch down, cupping around your chin with both hands and pulling you towards me, licking your lips as I join my tongue with yours, reverent at the pleasure it just delivered. You are so amazingly good at that, it's almost a crime for you to spend your time doing anything else. I kiss you hard on the mouth before dotting kisses along your chin to your ear and whispering "Thank you."

"Are you kidding me? The pleasure was all mine baby, you taste beautiful," you say, as you grab me up into your arms and throw me over your shoulder. I squeal as you spank my arse and practically run up the stairs with me.

"Bedroom?" you shout.

"Left, last door."

You push open the door with your side, crossing the room and throwing me onto the bed.

I push up on my elbows as you undo your belt and slide it out of your jeans teasingly, every inch, an inch closer to getting my hands onto your skin. My heart quickens at the very thought of it.

I struggle to breathe as you take off your t-shirt, the streetlamps outside offering enough light to see you clearly, and you look so fine. I'm light headed as you undo your fly and slip off your jeans, your tight grey boxers giving me my first proper glimpse of just how big you are, anticipation ripe in the air like static between us.

I sit up, impatient, running a hand up your inner thigh, teasing your balls through your boxers with my fingernails, inhaling your scent to commit to memory forever. I smile as I slide my fingers inside the waist band of your boxers and pull them down, releasing your cock from its confinement. Does that feel better?

It is a thing of beauty, standing proudly in front of me, pre-cum beading on the head, twitching slightly as I exhale, licking my lips and sticking out my tongue. I want to taste you so badly, feel your girth between my lips and sliding down my throat. I think you're big enough to choke me.

I spit, to moisten the head of your cock, nudging your foreskin back with my lips as I do, taking care not to move too fast too soon, despite my desperate need to devour you. Once your head is revealed I swirl my tongue across the tip and taste you fully.

Delicious.

I part my lips and slide you in, just enough to cover the tip, rolling my tongue around the head with you still enclosed, blowing hot air through my nose onto your shaft as I lap you some more, slow, and steady, just teasing the head.

Your groans signal your pleasure as you hold my shoulders loosely, rocking your body with every dip of my head. I look up at your face, your eyes are closed but your smile is clear. I grin before reaching up and stroking your balls, and you groan as your hands move to my hair, gripping tight at the base of my neck.

I concentrate on the head of your cock but increase my pace, flicking hard as I massage your balls and rake them with my fingernails. I lap down your shaft and revel in the salty taste of your skin, sucking a ball into my mouth lazily. I reach behind and grab your arse, scratching with my nails all the way to the back of your knees.

I pull away and grab hold of your cock so I can position it in my lips, and then sucking you deep into my mouth, my lips tight and stretching painfully as I take you all in, relaxing as best I can to accommodate you in my throat sucking hard and then sliding you back out, repeating again and again as your breath quickens and you start to sigh.

I want to swallow you deeper but you're just too big, so I spit on my hand and take most of your shaft in that, waking you into my mouth and concentrating my lips and tongue on your head. You look in ecstasy and murmur something as you watch me, but I'm making too much noise, slurping on your cock, to hear what it is.

Your body's tense, your hips swaying with every tug and lick I make, your hand tighter and tighter in my hair until it starts to hurt, but I like it and it makes me work faster and harder with my hand and mouth. I want to feel your cock explode in my mouth or shooting over my face and tits, but you pull away from my mouth with a sigh.

I question with my eyes.

"I want to fuck you so badly. I don't want to cum before I've fucked you," you whisper, pushing me back onto the bed and nestling your body between my thighs. I feel your cock against my leg and my cunt throbs with need. I want to feel you inside me right now. Want you to slide your full length into my dripping, waiting pussy.

Why aren't you fucking me already?

I bring my feet up onto your arse, stabbing you with my heels, and urge you move, gasping as I feel your cock at the entrance to my pussy, teasing me so deliciously.

"Oh please fuck me," I beg, but you don't seem in any kind of hurry to do as I ask, stroking hair from my face as you kiss me gently, sucking one of my lips into your mouth and biting as you release it.

"What's the rush?"

What's the rush? God, seriously? You're killing me here!

Kissing me again, this time harder, you rest your elbows either side of my head as you finger my hair, your kiss stoking the already raging fire in my pussy.

I run my hand down your back, and you smirk as I find a ticklish spot on your side. I resist the urge to tickle you more, instead running my hands up the muscles of your arms and over your shoulders as you tense to lean in and kiss me again, this time even harder than before, biting me harder and fighting your tongue with mine.

You go to pull away but I don't let you, grabbing around your neck with my arm to keep your lips on mine, bucking my hips up off the bed so I can feel your cock against my hole. I arch up harder, I need to have you inside me, and I can tell you're smirking, even while kissing me, as I try and force you to fuck me.

In frustration, I grip your body with my thighs, and you're not expecting it so I flip you easily, pushing down on your shoulders when you try to wrestle me back onto my back, but only half-heartedly and with a huge grin on your face.

"Taking charge are we?"

I nod, running my hand over your torso, stopping to tweak your nipples, gently at first and then harder when you sigh and tip back your head. I lean in kissing down your neck and lapping your chest, feeling your body jerk beneath my eager tongue. Flicking your nipple and biting it as I reach behind and take your cock in my hand, guiding it to my pussy which contracts at the thought of having you inside me.

Now it's my turn to tease you. I know my juice must be bathing the head of your cock as I tease you, then lower slowly, inch by inch. You're so big, you fill me completely, and I groan long and hard as our hips hit and your balls nestle between my arse cheeks.

I pause to savour the sensation of you filling me so completely. Your cock feels as though it was made to measure. Oh, I'm so gonna enjoy this.

I lean forward, resting my tits on your chest, and kiss you on the lips as I begin to move, just a subtle rock of my hips at first, milking you with my pussy as I rotate in circles, keeping you buried deep inside me, gripping your shaft tight as I move. A little bit faster now but still in circles, not lifting, just rotating to keep you within me as deep as possible, so deep and so much pleasure.

Pushing off your chest, and placing my hands on your shoulders, I rotate wider, alternating one way and then the other, lifting up until just your head remains in my pussy and then groaning as I slide back down your cock.

"Ahhh fuck that's good," you gasp, clutching at the duvet cover.

I lift off and slide back down again, slow and deliberate, my hands clutching and scratching at your chest, every stoke a little bit harder than the one before, but still taking my time. I don't want either

60

of us to cum just yet, I want to ride you as long as I can hold out. I want to feel you inside me until I can't remember what it feels like without you there.

You cock rubs the front wall of my pussy with every thrust, and it feels so good for me.

Does it feel as good for you right now?

I arch back, my hands now on your thighs, twisting so I can lift up and then slam down on you. I resist the urge to speed up even though I'm desperate too, my thighs starting to burn, my calves cramping and my shoulders tense.

Are you watching my tits bounce as I ride you? They look pretty good from where I am so they must look really good from where you are. You reach up and grab them, circling the nipples and then pulling until they're rock hard.

"mmmmmmmmmmmmmmmm," I let my head fall back. My hair must be brushing against your balls at this angle. Does that feel nice?

I snake my hips back and forth to ride you harder. In this position I can feel your cock grinding against my g-spot, but I need more stimulation on my clit to cum. I need to move.

You look disappointed for a second when I stop, lifting one leg so I can swivel, and winking back over my shoulder as I turn to face your toes.

"Like the view?"

You grin and nod, your hands walking up my back and resting on my shoulders.

I fuck you harder, grinding my hips against yours. I need to cum and right now I don't care about you, I just need to get off. My clit rubs against the hair on your balls increasing the pleasure, and it feels so fucking perfect as I ride you with everything I have in me, I know it's only going to take a few minutes like this.

My hands grip your thighs, my own painful. I growl, forcing my body to keep going, every muscle rigid, sweat dripping into my eyes, down my back and between my breasts. You bring your knees up and start to meet my every stroke with your own, your hands moving from my shoulders to my hips, yanking me down hard onto your cock as you buck up into me.

I can hardly get in enough breath and exhaustion is creeping in, but I have to keep going. I have to keep riding you until we've both cum. Nothing else matters right now.

Your legs look tense as you push up harder, and I wrap my hands around your knees resting my head against them, concentrating all of my energy to my hips and thighs, to keep them moving in the perfect rhythm we've established.

You twist slightly and stab my g-spot with your cock. "Oh God, there, fuck me there... harder, harder, fuck... harder, HARDER," I demand through gritted teeth, and you do as instructed, pulling me onto you, sliding your balls against my clit with each stroke. Oh that's it baby, keep doing that.

"Fuckkkkkkkkkkkkkkkkkkkkkkkkkkkkk."

I can't control my thighs as they clench around your hips, and I almost knock my chin against your knees as I lunge forwards, my pussy contracting around your cock.

Just a few more seconds...

"Oh God, I'm gonna cum so hard."

"That's it baby, I want to feel you cum on my cock."

"Ah... ah... ah." I tip back my head, "urghhhhhhhhhhhhhhhhhhhhhhhhhhhh."

It starts deep inside and feels like a hurricane, sweeping up everything in its path. My torso convulses, and it rips through my shoulders and arms, my legs shaking, my toes curling back and getting caught in the sheet, almost cramping.

You continue to fuck me hard as I cum, grabbing both of my arms to stop me falling forwards as you lower your legs, gripping around my tits with your forearm as you sit up and press your chest into my back, your chin hard into my shoulder, your breath deafening and frantic.

Your groans intensifying and I know you're close. I slam my pussy down onto your cock, I want this to be so good for you. I feel your legs tense and your arm grips tighter, and then you stop moving and groan. I close my eyes, so I'm not distracted from the feel of your cock spurting your hot spunk up inside me. I feel three twitches as your cock pumps, and I grip hard, so I can milk every last drop of cum from you.

My breath slows as I lean my head back against your shoulder, totally spent. Opening my eyes, I smile as I look at you. Your pleasure's clear on your face, your lips parted in a snarled grin, your eyes closed, your face flushed, your hair messed up.

We don't move as your cock softens and eventually slides out, followed by your cum, dripping onto your balls. You kiss my neck as our breath returns to normal, your arms now lose around my chest, the other stroking my hair.

You open your eyes looking completely fuck dazed, and I grin like a Cheshire cat. "That was the most amazing fuck I've ever had," I whisper, leaning in to kiss you.

And I mean every word.

Sweet Ass Candy

The red-head at the bar keeps looking in our direction. She's stunning, hair cut in a pixie crop, exposing the back of her neck with a small tattoo of wings, green eyes that seem to glow in the dim lights of the club, a tight arse in hot pants, shapely legs in knee high boots.

She turns again and I see enough of her breasts to know they're large, probably DD's at least. She chews her lip before sucking on her straw seductively. Picking a cherry out of her glass, she bites into it.

I feel your cock spasm in my hand as I stroke the shaft from base to tip. Your face is relaxed, calm even. It amazes me every time. How you can just sit there with a face like that while I wank your beautiful hard cock underneath the table?

I look back at the red-head with a smile. Does she know I'm massaging the head right now? Does she know your hand is deep inside my panties, rubbing my clit, every now and then plunging into my cunt and making me gasp, my hot wet juice dripping onto your wrist?

Her eyes tell me that she does, and she'd like to do a bit more than think about it. I move my fingers twisting the way you like it. I notice your hands tense a bit, and a waiver of pleasure crosses your face. This is when you like me to move in long hard strokes, build you up to a frenzy but keep you from going over the edge.

I change rhythm, strong, hard tugs, and you match me, plunging two fingers into my pussy and using your thumb on my clit. I have to lean an elbow on the table and cover my mouth to stop from crying out, and I see you smirk.

The red-head is still staring at us. I turn to you with a questioning look, and you nod, sighing as I release your cock and watch you stuff it back in your trousers. My pussy feels so empty when you withdraw your hand. You go to put it on the table, but I grab your wrist and bring it to my nose, the smell of my cunt driving me mad.

I turn to the redhead as I draw your fingers into my mouth, sucking off my own sweetness, all the while thinking about licking on her delicious breasts, and putting my mouth to her dark wet holes. I feel your body tense. Are you thinking the same thing? Perhaps you're thinking about fucking that hot little pussy of hers while I lick her clit? Either way, I see your cock straining against the confinement of your trousers.

The red-head points to herself and then over to us, and we both nod at her eagerly, turning to each other and grinning wide. Tonight is about to get a whole lot more interesting.

She saunters over, her hips swinging and her breasts bouncing. She's incredibly sexy, and I just can't wait for us to get her naked and pleasure her until she screams, but I think she'd like a bit of action here first and I'm guessing you'd like to give it to her as much as me.

I slide out of the booth and she squeezes in-between us.

"You up for some fun tonight…"

"Call me Candy."

We all laugh.

"Sure, if you like. You up for some fun tonight… Candy?" I ask her, and she nods, an eager look on her face.

I rest my hand on her knee under the table and you do the same and I see her body relax back into the chair. She's very up for some fun tonight.

We both trace our fingers up her inner thighs, the tight flesh buckling under mine as we do. I reach the edge of her hotpants. They're so tight against her cunt I can see the outline of her lips from where I'm sitting. I continue to stroke her thigh while you sneak a hand up inside.

She moans long and low as you start to stroke her clit with long strokes, just like you do with me. She writhes against you; she likes it as much as I do. I remove my hand from her leg and move my body, discreetly covering her breast from view of prying eyes, before pushing down her top to expose it. She's not wearing a bra so her beautiful pertness is on full display, her dark nipples already erect from your attention on her clit.

I tweak them between my fingers and she tips her head back, letting out a gasp. I circle the nipple with a finger, before sucking one into my mouth, and then stopping and doing the same again, leaning in to blow against it. You watch with fervour, your eyes darting between my fingers, rolling her nipple between them, and your hand working away at her clit.

She lets out a whimper. Have you stuck your fingers in her cunt? I look down to confirm my suspicions. I bet her pussy is tight and hot. I bet you're so hard right now, your cock demanding attention and needing to fuck something, anything, so badly it's starting to hurt. How much do you want to fuck us both right here and right now in front of everyone? Just bend one of us over the table and do us really hard? I'm guessing a lot.

Candy's breath is quick and sharp now. You're working her really furiously, a huge smile as you watch the pleasure you're causing her displayed fully on her face. I squeeze a handful of breast. I'm desperate to suck that beautiful huge bud of her nipple into my mouth. My pussy is dripping wet with excitement. I feel a tingle inside my belly and a deep throbbing ache rising up until I think it's going to swallow me whole.

I can't hold back. I lean in and take her nipple in my mouth, lapping my tongue over it like I'm devouring an ice cream.

Her hands grip the edge of the chair.

"I think she's ready to come baby." I say and you nod at me. She groans her approval. I turn my attention back to her nipple and bite it gently until her sounds tell me to bite it harder. Your hand is working her skilfully. Your fingers curled inside rubbing her g-spot no doubt, that spongy flesh that will get her so hot she's going to clamp down on your hand and grip your forearm with her thighs. The nub of your thumb is working her clit, circles and then sweeps. I love it when you do that. I love to feel your fingers working me so hard. She loves it too.

God, my pussy feels empty right now.

She bucks up off the chair against your arm hard and I know to clamp down on her nipple because she's gonna cum right now, right in front of everyone. Your hand buried deep inside that hot, slick wetness, and my teeth on her pert breast. She throws her head back with a groan as she cums, and you lean towards me as she does, kissing me hard on the lips, basking in the pleasure we've caused her together. I can't believe how horny I am right now. Are you as horny as I am? Are you as desperate and needy to have your own pleasure until you find release?

I tuck her breast back in her top and you take out your hand out of her hot pants, offering me your fingers to suck, which I do with pleasure. God, she tastes sweet.

"Do you want to continue this at ours?" you ask her.

"Hell yeah," she replies.

****

You're still dressed and sitting on a chair in the corner of the room. I know you're desperate for your cock to see some action, but I also know you love to be teased until that animalistic need overtakes you, that all-consuming urge to rip out your hard shaft and ram in into something.

Candy and I are naked now, lying on the bed facing each other. I stroke her. It's beautiful to feel her soft skin beneath my fingers, to run them over the curves of her gorgeous body, every now and again slipping them between her legs to graze her clit.

"What do you want me to do to your girl?" Candy asks you.

You sit up in the chair in excitement. Oh, she want's direction. I bet you're wondering how slick my pussy is right now, quivering with my imaginings.

"I want you to suck her tits first."

Candy pushes me back on the bed and climbs on top. I love the feel of her wet pussy against my stomach and you look as though you might shoot your load right there in your trousers as she bends over, her arse in your direction and takes my full breast into her mouth. Her mouth is hot and her tongue is skilled, flicking hard against my nipple. I groan both in pleasure and pain, my neglected pussy begging for some attention.

I spread my legs wide and you smile at me. What a beautiful view you must have, my hot pussy, glistening, slick with anticipation and thrill, and her tight little arsehole, being offered up to you like a prize as she works my breasts in her mouth.

You reach down and unzip your fly. Grabbing your cock in your hands and stroking it. Don't you want to fuck us? I look at you.

"I'm going to need to have a wank first or I won't last five minutes, the two of you are so hot together."

Candy smiles as she pushes up from my breasts and kisses me fully on the lips. Her tongue tastes of cherries and her lips are soft and sensuous. Our tongues dance together lazily, and she runs her fingers over my face and through my hair.

"Shall we give him a show while he wanks off over us?" Candy asks me. I nod. I like her style.

Candy climbs off and settles herself between my thighs, a hand on each leg and her head primed to deliver me something special. I begin to tremble.

"Do you want to come over my back?" Candy asks you. You struggle to get up off the chair your hard on is so huge, but you nod ripping off your trousers and top. You climb behind Candy and rub your cock up against her back before grabbing it in your hand and working it in a slow rhythm.

Candy offers me her tongue, lapping at my pussy like she's hungry. Her tongue's not as strong as yours but she knows how I like it, she must like it just the same as me. You'll have fun licking her out.

How's your view? I bet it's so hot watching Candy lick out my cunt, watching her tongue and lips cause me to push up against her face, to grind into her in pursuit of further pleasure. I bet you just want to ram that cock in either one of us right now? You won't though. Not yet.

I concentrate on your face. I know you're about to cum, your body arching to get the maximum grip on your cock, and I smile wide as your hot stream of spunk shoots out over Candy's back and you shout out your pleasure. I feel Candy gasp against me, probably at the sensation of you bathing her in your cream.

You're kind enough to wipe Candy down with a towel before lying down next to me. I love that spent look in your eyes combined with excitement as Candy works me, her mouth being joined by her fingers.

"Fuck," I mutter as I arch up against her.

You lean in and kiss me, our tongues furious in each other's mouths. "Cum for me baby," you whisper in my ear and the shivers it sends me, combined with Candy's skill cause me to explode in a powerful orgasm. My whole body convulsing, my thighs gripping around Candy's head and my tongue entwined with yours.

I stroke Candy's hair in thanks as she emerges from between my legs, covered in my slippery wetness. You release me from your kiss as she climbs up my body and takes over, the salty sweetness of my cum, intoxicating. Then she turns to you and offers you her face and I watch you lick the traces of me from it before merging your lips and tongue with hers.

Pushing back from me you allow her to nestle in the middle of us and we embrace each other over her, all needing to rest for a while.

****

I hear a groan, I think I dozed off. I open my sleepy eyes to see Candy, head back, biting down on her hand. Sitting up on my elbows, I see your head buried deep within her thighs and she's enjoying it a lot. I roll onto my side, rubbing down your back with my foot, and you look up at me and grin before returning your attention back to her pussy. I know how good she tastes, how much your enjoying lapping at that dark hole, how your loving the way she grinding up at you, begging you without words to stick your tongue in deeper, to sweep that clit just a little bit harder, to build her up to a point she can't return from and then push her over the edge. I'm surprised when you pull back and stop. She lets out a disappointed sigh.

Your cock is rock hard and twitching as you move towards me licking your lips. I spread my legs wide for you. How does my pussy look right now? Is it begging you to lick it clean? Does it look like it needs a good hard pounding?

You move to me, but not in a rush. You lick up my body taking my huge breast in your mouth, working your tongue on one nipple and your fingers on the other. Candy's watching, stroking her clit, every now and again her fingers pleasuring deep inside her.

Licking your way back down you breathe hard on my pussy, licking and then breathing, licking and then drawing in cold air across my skin. It makes me shudder at the intensity of the sensation. You smile against my hot wetness because you love it when I can't control my body. When you get me so excited my limbs twitch.

"Would you like to suck off my man for a bit?" I ask Candy, and she smiles obligingly.

I watch her move over towards you laying face up between your legs. The bed's not long enough for her to stretch out completely but she manages to squeeze in anyhow. I watch you lower your cock into her mouth. I bet that feels good, her hot little mouth tight around your cock. She gags a bit as you push it in fully, but she doesn't resist you, sucking you into her completely.

How good does that feel? To have your cock buried into her mouth while you press your tongue up against my cunt and lick me hard. To be pleasured and give pleasure at the same time. You start to groan hard. I wonder if she's flicking her tongue over the tip, slurping you long, good and hard. I hear the slapping sounds of her lips against you and it makes me so hot, to think of how much fun you must be having right now.

You push away from me. "I'm sorry baby but I need to fuck something now," you sigh and I giggle at you. I bet you do. I bet you've needed to fuck something for quite a long time. You've done well to hold out as long as you have.

"Who do you want to fuck?" I ask. I'm fine either way.

Candy's eyes grow wide. She wants to have you inside her real bad, and I don't blame her you're a really, really good fuck.

"By all means," I say to her and you look so excited.

"How do you want me?" Candy asks.

"On your back first," you growl at her. God you're horny right now. You're eyes are glazed with lust and your limbs are trembling a little. You're really excited about fucking a tight new pussy, one you've never fucked before, new and unchartered territory that your shaft longs to invade and then conquer.

She does as she's instructed and you climb on top of her. You plunge your hard cock deep inside, and she cries out, at its length no doubt, because you're hung like a horse. I run my fingers down your back as you fuck her. You're moving slowly, you must not want it to end. You must just want to keep on doing this forever. The look on her face tells me she feels exactly the same way.

I reach back to the bedside cabinet and grab the lube, smearing it on my fingers. Your butt is clenched tight as you thrust away in her, but I manage to sneak my fingers in-between your sweet arse cheeks and tentatively probe your hole. I push in gently against the resistance until my finger slides in completely and I wiggle it and slide it in and out.

"Fuck baby, you know how I like it," you cry out. I push harder even though it's really difficult keeping in time with your thrusts. To be in her tight pussy and have my finger deep in your arse, are you ready to cum yet?

You stop moving. "Baby will you fuck me with a strap on?" you ask, a desperate look on your face.

I chuckle. "How could I refuse you?"

You pull out of Candy and roll her over, positioning her up on her knees.

I take out our strap ons and you choose the smaller one, you must be so ready to explode you can't handle anything else. I secure it to my hips and you lick your lips.

I kneel behind as you offer your arse to me. I lap at it, sticking the tip of my tongue inside. I watch your back tense as I rim you just the way you like it. Sticking my finger back in I stretch you, before adding another finger and then another, opening you up ready for the strap on to drive home. I lube it up and push it against you, teasing you with it. Are you scared right now? Do you love the moment just before

71

I push it in? The anticipation of being filled fully, with all the pleasure and pain that entails.

I ease into you gently. I have to use a lot of force but you're relaxed and resigned to my deep intrusion. How does that feel right now? I bet it feels really good. I move forwards clamped to you as you stick your cock back in Candy's slick cunt. I can imagine how good that feels, to feel her tightness around your cock and the pain of the strap-on ramming your behind.

You grab hold of Candy's hips as I grab hold of yours. It's hard to keep our momentum the same but I do the best I can, and you're vocal in your appreciation of both mine and Candy's efforts to bring you to climax. You start to ram into her harder and faster and I struggle to keep up with you. Now it's her turn to vocalise her enjoyment.

"That's it do me real hard," she cries back at you. My pussy is gagging for something filling it but I'm happy just to be ramming into your behind with this strap on. I love to make you feel good. It fills me with pleasure to imagine how amazing this feels for you.

Candy cums with a scream as you pound into her and rub her clit, and I feel every muscle in your body clench. You like to save your spunk for me, so you pull out as you start to cum, shooting your cream all over her arse with the strap on still buried deep inside you. I bet that's the best orgasm you've ever had. Every part of your body dragged into the spasms that engulf you.

Candy falls to the bed beneath you. Her hair wet and pressed to her face, her body dripping in sweat from the hard pounding you just delivered. You whimper as I pull out the strap on and remove it, throwing it onto the floor.

You flop onto the bed, dazed as you look up at me. I expect you want to make me cum because you know how desperate and horny I am, but you look exhausted right now. I lick some of your cream off Candy's arse before wiping the rest away.

You watch silently as she dresses, stopping every now and again to kiss me or you. She waves goodbye as she leaves the bedroom and I show her to the door.

"Your guys the best fuck ever. I envy you," she smiles, kissing me again as she wanders off down the path, and I close the door behind her.

You're fast asleep when I get back to the bedroom. I guessed as much. I don't mind because I know full well how horny you'll be when you wake up. You'll make it up to me later. I'll make sure of it.

Lightning Source UK Ltd.
Milton Keynes UK
UKOW052008280612

195211UK00002B/167/P